GROUNDED

We walked down the Jetway to the aircraft's main door where a police officer stood. George indicated for me to wait as he disappeared into the flight deck. A few minutes later, he poked his head out and motioned for me to join him. Up to that moment, I'd been anxious to accompany him into the cockpit, but I was now hesitant. His raised eyebrows said, "Either come or stay, Jessica. Don't prolong this."

I joined him in the cockpit and looked inside. The lighting was dim, but even in the shadowy illumination I saw the figure of a person in the captain's seat. It was the body of Wayne Silverton. George took a few steps into the area, and I followed. Now the scene was clearer, and tragically real. Silverton's lifeless form was slumped forward over the pilot's control yoke, his weight pushing it fully forward. . . .

Coffee, Tea, or Murder?

A *Murder, She Wrote* Mystery

A NOVEL BY
JESSICA FLETCHER & DONALD BAIN

Based on the Universal television series created by
Peter S. Fischer, Richard Levinson & William Link

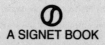

A SIGNET BOOK

SIGNET
Published by New American Library, a division of
Penguin Group (USA) Inc., 375 Hudson Street,
New York, New York 10014, USA
Penguin Group (Canada), 90 Eglinton Avenue East, Suite 700, Toronto,
Ontario M4P 2Y3, Canada (a division of Pearson Penguin Canada Inc.)
Penguin Books Ltd., 80 Strand, London WC2R 0RL, England
Penguin Ireland, 25 St. Stephen's Green, Dublin 2,
Ireland (a division of Penguin Books Ltd.)
Penguin Group (Australia), 250 Camberwell Road, Camberwell, Victoria 3124,
Australia (a division of Pearson Australia Group Pty. Ltd.)
Penguin Books India Pvt. Ltd., 11 Community Centre, Panchsheel Park,
New Delhi - 110 017, India
Penguin Group (NZ), 67 Apollo Drive, Rosedale, North Shore 0632,
New Zealand (a division of Pearson New Zealand Ltd.)
Penguin Books (South Africa) (Pty.) Ltd., 24 Sturdee Avenue,
Rosebank, Johannesburg 2196, South Africa

Penguin Books Ltd., Registered Offices:
80 Strand, London WC2R 0RL, England

First published by Signet, an imprint of New American Library,
a division of Penguin Group (USA) Inc.

First Printing, April 2007
10 9 8 7 6 5 4

For our editor, Kerry Donovan, who
makes our books better.

And to today's flight attendants, who face
the possibility of crazed terrorists, and the reality
of fed-up, angry air travelers every day they
come to work. Our hats are off to you.

Chapter One

"We are about to embark on a new and exciting era in commercial aviation. The days of passengers having their knees jammed into their chins and three-dollar bags of pretzels are over. Today marks the introduction of a sensible and civilized approach to air travel. Passengers on SilverAir will be treated like human beings; people who are willing to spend a little more—and I stress 'a little more'—can travel in comfort and style. I am extremely gratified that all of you are here today to help launch SilverAir. I see many friends who are ready to experience this new dimension in air travel, and for the press who will travel with us—well, I hope you'll write nice things about SilverAir."

A few members of the press laughed as Wayne Silverton, founder and chairman of SilverAir, stepped down from the portable podium that had been erected next to the freshly painted, sky blue 767-200 jet aircraft with the name of the airline emblazoned in silver on both sides and vertically on the stabilizer. The occasion was SilverAir's inaugural flight from Boston's Logan International Airport to England's Stansted International Airport, an increasingly popular airport in the UK for start-up airlines. Located forty-five miles northeast of London, it had become the third busiest airport in the UK—home to forty airlines and handling more than twenty million passengers a year. Arriving there would be a new experience for me. On my many trips to London, Heathrow had been my destination airport. But I always enjoy deviations from the norm when traveling, and flying on Wayne Silverton's airline, to a different airport, certainly represented that.

Because the aircraft was parked in a specially designated spot at the airport, away from the main terminal with its Jetway access to planes, we boarded by going up a set of stairs that had been rolled into place. Wayne and his wife, Christine, stood at the foot of the stairs and personally welcomed each passenger.

"Ah, Jessica," Wayne said, flashing his characteristic broad, brilliant smile. He was a stunningly attractive man by any standard, his perpetually tanned square face providing a contrasting background for very white teeth. "I am so glad that you could find the time in your busy schedule to help us celebrate this special day."

"I wouldn't have missed it for the world," I said.

"How exciting to be a guest on a new airline's maiden flight."

"I never thought this day would come," Christine said.

She was as beautiful as her husband was handsome. Christine had been a stewardess for Pan Am until that proud airline eventually went under. Of course, by the time that happened, stewardesses were no longer referred to by that name. They became known as flight attendants, the change having mostly to do with an influx of males working flights. You couldn't very well refer to them as "stewardesses." But no matter what they were called, I've always had a special fondness and respect for the men and women who make their living at thirty-thousand feet, keeping passengers happy, but most important assuring the safety of those in their charge, particularly when emergencies crop up. Fortunately, that was a rare occurrence in modern commercial aviation.

"You must be bursting with pride," I said.

"And exhaustion," Christine replied, the smile never leaving her finely chiseled, classically beautiful face. "But all the hard work was worth it, especially having so many of Wayne's friends from Cabot Cove with us this morning."

Wayne Silverton had been born and raised in Cabot Cove, Maine. A standout high school athlete—football, basketball, and track—he went to Purdue University on a full scholarship, majoring in aeronautical engineering, a discipline for which that Indiana university is well-known. It was assumed that he would forge a career in engineering, which was where he started out after serving three years as an officer in the air force. He was hired by Pan Am and quickly rose through its ranks to become executive vice president of that once dominant airline, which was where he met, and wooed, Christine. But an indomitable entrepreneurial spirit had taken hold of him, and he left the airline to join a well-financed real estate consortium that bought a series of small, unprofitable casinos and hotels in Las Vegas. The group renovated them into attractive properties, resulting in their sale for many millions more than the group had paid. Those deals made Wayne a rich man, and he left that real estate partnership to form his own construction company, building high-rise condominiums in that gambling Mecca. Unfortunately, he was ahead of the curve; it would be years before the condominium craze in Vegas caught hold. According to what I read in the business press, Wayne eventually fell on hard times, and it was rumored that he was on the brink of bankruptcy.

A few years later, I was surprised, and delighted, to read that he'd put together financing to launch a new airline, SilverAir. Shortly after that announcement, he and Christine returned to Cabot Cove to bask in the accolades thrown his way—local boy makes good, again—and to tout the airline to local civic and professional groups. That's when I renewed

my acquaintance with him and Christine, and I'd followed the progress of his start-up airline leading to
the day when I, along with others from the town,
received an invitation to join a group of dignitaries,
members of the press, and friends on the upstart airline's maiden voyage to England.

"But you are going, aren't you?" I said to my
friend of many years, Dr. Seth Hazlitt, who'd also
received an invitation from Wayne Silverton.

"I can't say I'm much inclined," he replied. "You
know I've never been a fan of flying. Bad enough on
one of the big, established airlines. But this one is
brand spankin' new. Might be smart to wait till
they've gotten the kinks out."

"It doesn't seem to me that being new means
much," Mort Metzger, our sheriff, chimed in. We
were having breakfast together at Mara's, our favorite local eatery down at the Cabot Cove dock. "I'm
sure Silverton wouldn't get involved with anything
unsafe."

"You're just parroting what Maureen says," Seth
said. "I'm sure she's chompin' at the bit to go. Your
wife is always up for going somewhere."

"She's adventurous, that's true," Mort said,
"but—"

"Wayne Silverton was always a little too slick for
my taste," Seth said, spearing the final piece of blueberry pancake on his plate. "Made his money out in
Las Vegas. Sounds a bit fishy to me."

"It's a big city, Doc. Lots of people make money there," Mort said.

"There may have been times he had to be 'slick,' as you term it, Seth, to have been so successful in business," I said in Wayne's defense. "Big business can be cutthroat."

"Well," Seth said, patting his mouth with his napkin and leaning back in his seat, "be that as it may, I'll have to give this inaugural flight business a little more thought."

Mara, who'd been busy in the kitchen, came to the table, a pot of coffee in her hand. She topped off Mort's cup. "I've got another pot of decaf brewing," she said to Seth and me. "Everything else to your satisfaction?"

"Always is," Mort said.

"So?" Mara asked, taking in the three of us. "Are you going to Boston to be on SilverAir's first flight?"

"Looks like Mrs. F., Maureen, and I are," Mort replied. "Doc, here, he's not so sure."

"He just likes to be convinced. Isn't that right, Doc?" Mara gave me a sly wink.

Seth grunted but didn't reply.

"You couldn't get me on one of those things for all the money in the world," she said.

"You've never flown, Mara?" Mort asked.

"Never have, never will. Don't see any wings on this back, do you? Until you do, I'll stay right here. Man wasn't made to fly."

"He wasn't made to drive, either, Mara," Seth said, "but I notice you get around town in a car."

"That's different," she said, taking Seth's plate before he could scrape up the last bit of syrup with his fork.

The bell over the door rang, and we all turned as Cabot Cove's mayor, Jim Shevlin, entered the luncheonette.

"Good morning, Your Honor," Seth said as Shevlin pulled up a chair.

"Good morning, all," Shevlin said. To Mara: "A dry English muffin, if you don't mind, and—"

"A bowl of fruit," she finished for him. "Be right back."

"On a diet?" Mort asked.

"I'm always on a diet," the mayor said. "So, I understand you've all been invited on SilverAir's first trip, too."

"That's right," I said.

"Susan and I are really looking forward to it," Shevlin said. "It was nice of Wayne to remember his Cabot Cove roots, especially since we haven't seen the man in a few years, except in the news recently every now and then. Jenkins and Marterella were invited and are going, too." Richard Jenkins and Sal Marterella were members of our city council. "Lucky for us Silverton doesn't do any business with the town, so there's no conflict. I understand there were some state officials on the invite list, but they turned

7

him down. Still, Maine'll be well represented. Jed Richardson told me he and the missus plan on making the flight." Jed was a former airline pilot who'd retired, returned to Cabot Cove with his wife, Barbara, and established his own small charter airline, as well as a flight school. I'd taken flying lessons from him and earned my private pilot's license.

Mort and I looked at Seth. I said, "How can you not join everyone, Seth?"

Mort said, "Silverton'll feel insulted if Cabot Cove's leading physician turns him down."

"I said I'd think about it and I will," Seth said, standing and laying money on the table. "Right now I've got me a waiting room full of patients who need"—he looked down at Mort—"who need Cabot Cove's leading physician. Good day, everyone."

I went up the steps leading into the 767 aircraft, followed by Seth Hazlitt, the Metzgers, the Shevlins, and other guests invited to experience the new airline on its first commercial flight to London.

A flight attendant dressed in a silver jumpsuit with blue accessories welcomed us aboard.

"What a stunning uniform," I told her.

"Isn't it beautiful?" she said, turning to allow me to view it from another angle. "Wayne—Mr. Silverton—hired top Italian designers. I feel like a movie star in it."

I laughed. "And you look like one, too," I said. The name on her ID tag read GINA MOLNARI. I didn't know her nationality, but she could have given the most glamorous of Italian and Greek actresses a run for their money where looks were concerned. Her eyes were large and dark. Her smooth skin was a light olive color, her hair pitch black. And her outfit looked as though it had been tailored to perfectly fit her decidedly female form.

She greeted Seth, who was directly behind me, and I walked ahead to take in the aircraft's interior. It looked vastly different than any commercial airliner I'd been on in the past few years. The wide-body jet hadn't been configured into different classes. There was no partition for a first class or business class compartment. Instead the spacious interior was wide open and contained far fewer seats than was usual. A second flight attendant, as attractive as the first, said after reading my name tag, "Just a hundred and two seats, Mrs. Fletcher. Plenty of room to stretch out and enjoy the flight."

"It certainly looks comfortable," I said, continuing to inspect my surroundings. A great deal of money had obviously been spent designing and creating the single-class cabin. Everything was silver and blue, with small, tasteful touches of red to add visual contrast.

"Take any seat," the flight attendant said. "There are no assigned seats on this special flight."

The 102 seats in the spacious cabin were designed to swivel so that four people could create a conversation area. Seth, the Metzgers, and I manipulated them into that arrangement and sat to look through the packet of reading material that had been left on each seat. I glanced up at a video extolling SilverAir, which ran on state-of-the-art screens suspended from the ceiling.

Once we had settled into our seats, a third flight attendant, this one a young man wearing a masculine variation of what the women wore, came to offer drinks. "My name's John Slater," he said pleasantly. He was a good-looking fellow, of medium build, slender, with large, sensuous eyes, and wavy dark brown hair that fell softly over his brow. "I'll be one of your flight attendants for this flight."

"Wonderful meeting you," I said. "This is very exciting, being on a maiden flight."

"I'm excited, too," he said, giving forth with an engaging smile. "I'm really happy to be working for SilverAir. I think passengers are going to come aboard as happy campers." He laughed. "That's not the case with the last airline I worked for. Hundreds of angry people on every flight. Mr. Silverton has the right idea: Charge a little more and give a lot more. Welcome aboard."

We all ordered juices; it was a little too early in the day for anything stronger.

The cabin quickly filled up. Spirits were high, and there were a lot of "oohs" and "aahs" as people reacted to the posh cabin. Because we would be in London for only two nights, people had brought a minimal amount of luggage and stowed most of it in overhead bins. Maureen Metzger, however, who was affectionately known to friends who traveled with her as the "Luggage Queen," had packed as though we'd be away for two weeks, much to Mort's chagrin, although he was a good sport about it.

"Pretty nice plane, huh, Doc?" Mort said. "Glad you decided to come along?"

"It doesn't matter how pretty it is, Mort. What counts are those two engines hanging from the wings. And I'll tell you how glad I am at the end of the trip, if they function correctly and we land safely."

As drinks were being served, Wayne Silverton moved through the cabin, chatting with his guests and making everyone feel at home. He stopped to speak with us. As he did, I looked past him to where his wife, Christine, was engaged in an animated, I'd even say angry, conversation with the flight attendant who'd greeted us as we boarded. I couldn't make out their words, but it was evident that Christine was not happy with something the beautiful Gina had said or done. Christine straightened her back and turned sharply in our direction, with her features relaxed back into a serene expression, a smile on her lips. The flight attendant, however, couldn't cover her emotions so swiftly. She fixed Christine's retreating form with a hateful stare.

Oh, my, I thought as I returned my attention to Wayne, who was spouting forth on his determination to fix what was wrong with commercial aviation.

"We'll talk more once we're airborne," he said. "Wouldn't want to hold up the departure. We're anticipating a very smooth flight. Sit back and enjoy the trip. You're about to experience air travel the way it used to be—and should be."

No turbulence expected outside, I thought, and with a bit of luck we would have the same conditions aboard. I hoped the exchange between the two women wouldn't prove me wrong.

Chapter Two

Because the aircraft wasn't parked at a gate, there was no need to have it pushed back. The powerful twin jet engines came to life, and we inched forward in the direction of our assigned taxiway and runway. I was looking out the window at other aircraft when Wayne suddenly appeared again.

"What's this I hear from Jed Richardson that you're a pilot, Jessica?" he asked.

I laughed. "I do have my private pilot's license."

"She can fly a plane all right," said Seth, "but still doesn't have a driver's license."

I responded with feigned indignation. "I'll have you know that I am fully licensed to operate any bicycle with two wheels."

"Tell you what, Jessica," Silverton said. "How would you like to sit up front during takeoff?"

"In the cockpit?"

"Yup. Give you a great view, and you can watch the pros up there in action."

"You lucky thing," Maureen Metzger said.

"Don't pass this up," said Mort.

"Wonderful," I said, undoing my seat belt and following Wayne to the locked door that led to the flight deck.

"Mrs. Fletcher will be using the jump seat up front during takeoff," Wayne told the flight attendant, who sat in a small seat that pulled down from the wall. She unsnapped her seat belt and used a key to open the door, causing the captain and his first officer to turn.

"This is Jessica Fletcher, the famous mystery writer," Wayne said in a voice loud enough to override the engine noise. "She's also a pilot. I thought she'd enjoy watching the takeoff from up here."

The captain, a heavyset man with close-cropped gray hair, didn't look especially pleased with the suggestion. He grunted and pointed to a small seat directly behind him, which I knew was used for airline check pilots, FAA officials, or off-duty pilots hitching a ride back home. Having a civilian outsider in the cockpit was evidently okay, since this was a special promotional flight and the request came from the airline's owner. Under normal circumstances, and especially after the tragedy of Nine Eleven, the notion would have been unthinkable.

I settled into my assigned seat, secured my seat belt, and watched wide-eyed as the two-man cockpit crew skillfully maneuvered the huge plane to its assigned location on the busy field. The first officer, considerably younger than the captain, seemed to be doing most of the work. After completing a rundown of the preflight checklist, he looked back at me, smiled, and said, "Welcome to the flight deck. We should have a smooth flight for most of the trip."

"I'm looking forward to every minute of it," I replied.

"Now that we've got a real pilot aboard, maybe you'd like to switch seats with me and handle the takeoff."

I laughed and said, "Careful. I might lose my mind and take you up on it."

He returned to his duties, and the captain turned to me and said, "Welcome aboard, Mrs. Fletcher. Don't listen to Carl here. He'll do anything to get out of working."

"Carl Scherer," the first officer said over his shoulder. "Pleased to meet you, ma'am."

"My wife's a fan of your books, probably has every one of them," the captain said.

"I'm always happy to hear that," I said, pleased that his initial gruff demeanor had softened.

"Name's Caine, Bill Caine," he said, managing to reach around his seat back to shake my hand.

"Thank you," I said, "for allowing me this experience."

"What do you fly?" he asked.

"Nothing as big as this bird," I replied. "I have all my hours in a Cessna 172."

"Love that plane," he said. "I own one myself, fly it on weekends."

"A busman's holiday."

"That's *real* flying, Mrs. Fletcher. Up here we pretty much sit back and let the computers do the work. I fly my Cessna on my time off to stay honest. Why don't you put on those headphones and listen in to the tower and traffic control."

I did as he suggested. I knew that preparing for a takeoff or landing was the busiest time for pilots. In fact, regulations prohibited any conversation in the cockpit that wasn't directly related to the tasks at hand. I listened as Captain Caine and First Officer Scherer ran down an extensive checklist of pretakeoff items, and conversed over the radio in a shorthand unique to pilots. Their crisp professionalism was a joy to witness.

We pulled behind a line of other aircraft awaiting permission to take to the active runway, and slowly moved up in line as plane after plane took off before us. We were second in line when the first officer pointed to a small light amidst the myriad dials, switches, gauges, and buttons of the control panel. It wasn't illuminated. After some terse back-and-forth about the light, Captain Caine said, "Let's take her back." With that, he informed the control tower of a problem with the aircraft and that we were returning to the terminal for maintenance.

"We'll have to have this checked out," he said, turning to me.

"Not serious, I hope," I said.

"Probably just a burnt-out bulb, but I don't take anything for granted."

Nor should you, I silently agreed. *I wouldn't.*

The captain got on the plane's internal PA system and announced, "Ladies and gentlemen, this is Captain Caine from the flight deck. We've got what appears to be a minor problem with the aircraft and are returning to the terminal to have it checked out. Sorry for the inconvenience. Hopefully, the maintenance folks will straighten it out quickly and we can be on our way."

As the 767 turned away from the runway and began its lumbering trip back to where the problem could be rectified, Gina Molnari opened the cockpit door and poked her head in. Immediately, Wayne Silverton took her place, pushing her out of the way.

"What the hell is going on?" Silverton asked angrily.

Scherer explained about the light not functioning while Captain Caine continued to guide the plane.

"It's probably just a two-dollar bulb," Silverton said. "Let's get going."

"Sorry," Caine said, "but we don't go anywhere as long as that light doesn't come on."

"That's ridiculous," Silverton said in what could only be described as a snarl. "I've got a hundred VIPs back there, including plenty of press."

"I don't care if you've got the president of the United States," Caine said, never looking up at Silverton. "This plane is under my command, and I say it's a no-go until maintenance checks it out."

"I'm telling you that I own this airline," Silverton said, barely able to control his anger.

"And I'm telling you, Mr. Silverton, that as captain on this flight, I make the decisions, not you."

"We'll see about that when we get to London," Silverton snapped.

He'd been speaking as though I wasn't there. But he suddenly seemed to recognize my presence. He managed a small smile for my benefit and stormed from the flight deck.

"I'd better get back with the others," I said, hanging the headphones I'd been using on a hook and unbuckling my seat belt.

"Sorry for the delay," Captain Caine said. "Careful walking back to your seat."

My friends were filled with questions after I'd rejoined them in the passenger cabin.

"Nothing major," I assured them. "A little light that was supposed to come on didn't. I'm sure they'll have it fixed in no time."

I glanced at Seth, whose expression wasn't happy. I patted his hand. "Not to worry," I told my friend. "We're in good hands."

My prognosis was sound. A two-man maintenance crew arrived and spent fifteen minutes on the flight deck. They left, and Captain Caine came on the PA. "Looks like the problem has been fixed and we're ready to roll. Again, sorry for the delay. We'll make up for any lost time en route. We've got strong tail-winds forecast, which should get us to London ahead of schedule even with this late start. I'll get back to you once we're up at cruising altitude. If Mrs. Fletcher wants to come back up here for the takeoff, she's welcome."

One of the flight attendants escorted me to the flight deck, and I again took my privileged seat. This time, everything went smoothly. We roared down the runway until we'd reached a point at which aborting the takeoff would be unwise. The first officer called out in a loud voice, "V-One," indicating that we'd reached that spot where there wasn't enough runway left to be able to safely stop the jet. No matter what happened next, the takeoff had to be continued, even if an engine had failed. Sophisticated aircraft like the 767 are certified to take off on one engine if necessary.

"Rotate," was Scherer's next call. Based upon many factors preprogrammed into the onboard computers, this was the moment when the aircraft had gained the necessary speed to lift off. Captain Caine pulled back on the yoke, the landing gear broke free of the runway, and we were airborne. It was exhilarating to be up there on the flight deck while this was happening, an experience I would not soon forget. Taking off in a small, private plane is exciting for me, too, but the sheer power of the 767, and the choreographed coordination between the captain and the first officer, gave flight special meaning for me at that moment.

I remained there until we'd reached our cruising altitude of thirty-five thousand feet over the Atlantic, thanked Captain Caine, and returned to the passenger cabin. Jed Richardson, owner of our Cabot Cove air service, took my place in the cockpit.

There was a festive air among the passengers. The flight attendants had started serving drinks again the minute we left the ground, and it seemed as though a few of the passengers had already consumed too much. Seth and I ended up chatting with a couple of business writers from Boston and New York newspapers.

"What do you think of Wayne Silverton's idea of how to run an airline?" one of them asked us.

"Makes sense to me," Seth replied. "Unless you can afford to fly first class, those other airlines cram you in like sardines. This is a lot more comfortable." He indicated the cabin with a sweep of his hand.

"How about you, Mrs. Fletcher?"

"I agree with Dr. Hazlitt," I said. "Of course, according to what I've read, a passenger who usually flies coach will have to pay more to fly to London on SilverAir than on, say, British Airways or American Airlines. But as Wayne stresses, not that much more. I suspect there are millions of people who'll be willing to pay a little extra for this sort of comfort."

We gravitated to other groups as the flight attendants continued to deliver drinks and an array of hors d'oeuvres—caviar on small white crackers, cold shrimp, hot lamb skewers, and other tasty snacks. Soft jazz played through speakers. It had become one big party, and I wondered whether there was the possibility of it getting out of hand. But an announcement by a flight attendant put my mind at rest: "Ladies and gentlemen, please take your seats. We'll be serving dinner shortly."

It took a while for everyone to comply, but eventually all the seats were filled, although many passengers had chosen to change places in order to talk with others. As the flight attendants went about their predinner chores, I saw Wayne going from group to group, introducing another man. He eventually arrived where I sat with Seth and the two reporters; Mort and Maureen had temporarily joined another four-seat configuration with Mayor Shevlin and his wife, Susan.

"Mrs. Fletcher, Dr. Hazlitt, I'd like you to meet one of my partners in SilverAir, Sal Casale."

Mr. Casale was of medium height and compactly built: It wouldn't have surprised me if he spent a portion of each day in a gymnasium. He was a handsome man in a crude way. His coal black hair was combed straight back. He wore an obviously expensive black suit, a dazzling white-on-white shirt with a large, high collar, and a muted pale yellow tie. He had an exaggerated old-world courtly manner, his speech somewhat reminiscent of actors I remember from *The Godfather* movies. I judged him to be in his fifties.

"I understand you're a famous doctor," he said to Seth after introductions had been made.

"Afraid not," Seth answered. "I'm just a local chicken-soup doctor. The only famous person here is Mrs. Fletcher."

"That's right," Casale said. "The writer. I can never understand how anybody can write books. I get all tangled up even writing a letter."

"We all do what we do," I said brightly. "I write books, and you own an airline."

"Sal owns *part* of an airline," Wayne corrected.

Casale laughed. "Wayne, here, never lets me forget I'm just a partner." He leaned close to us and spoke in a conspiratorial voice. "You know what I think? I think owning an airline is pretty dumb. You know any airlines that make money these days? I don't."

"SilverAir will be the exception to the rule, Sal," Wayne said, a slight edge to his voice. "JetBlue and Southwest do all right, but we'll top them."

"We'd better," Casale said, straightening.

"Sal and I did some real estate deals together in Las Vegas," Wayne said, seeming to want to change the subject. "He's not my only partner in SilverAir. You'll meet my British colleagues when we get to London."

"Nice meeting you," Casale said and walked away.

Wayne smiled, shrugged, and said, "Enjoy your

dinner. The chateaubriand is prime, carved seat-side like it used to be in the good old days of flying."

Dinner was wonderful. I've never understood people who complain about airline food, at least the way it used to be before deregulation and the demise of airlines in this country. To me, whenever I flew and was served dinner, I considered it a miracle of sorts to be served a hot meal of any kind while flying at thirty-five thousand feet in an aluminum cigar tube known as an airplane. Of course, those days have changed, except for those fortunate enough to fly first class, particularly on some of the international airlines for whom passenger service still ranks as a top priority.

After dinner had been cleared, and as a popular movie was about to start on the video screens, I headed for a forward lavatory that was adjacent to the galley where the flight attendant, Ms. Molnari, was cleaning up. The lavatory was occupied, so I passed the time chatting with her.

"Will every SilverAir flight serve such an elaborate meal?" I asked.

"Afraid not, although each flight will feature a hot, three-course meal. Wayne—Mr. Silverton—pulled out all the stops for this special flight."

"It certainly makes for a pleasant trip," I said. "Did you work for another airline before joining SilverAir?"

"Sure. We all did. Christine, um, I mean Mrs. Sil-

23

verton, was with Pan Am, but I wasn't lucky enough to have worked for an airline like that."

"Did many people apply for a job with SilverAir?"

"Loads. As the airline expands, I'm sure lots more will be hired."

"You must enjoy your work, traveling the globe and meeting so many interesting people."

"It's not so glamorous anymore," she said, and added with a chuckle, "The *Coffee, Tea, or Me?* era is over. The good old days. Of course, I haven't been doing it as long as a lot of gals have. Like Christine. She goes way back—and loves to flaunt it."

"Oh?"

"Forget I said that," she quickly corrected. "Excuse me." She disappeared into the passenger cabin.

The rest of the flight was uneventful. Some passengers slept; others watched a second movie. Mort, Maureen, and Seth dozed off, leaving me to read a book I'd started before coming to Boston. I enjoy being secluded in the air without modern conveniences like a telephone or my computer to interfere, the whine of the jet engines the only intruder. It's prime reading time for me and I always try to take advantage of it.

I took a break at one point for a walk around the cabin to stretch my legs, something I always try to do on every flight. I dislike sitting in one place for too long and take frequent breaks when working on a novel at home. Whether I am chained to a computer or an airline passenger seat, moving about on a regular basis is a necessity, at least for me.

"Can I get you something?" one of the flight attendants asked from the galley.

"Thank you, no," I said. "Just getting the blood moving."

"Did you enjoy being up front?" she asked. She was a short, chunky young woman with beautifully coifed blond hair and a smile that would melt metal. As we spoke, she went about her work, opening and closing compartments, putting service items away, and taking out packets of coffee and bottled water.

"I loved it," I said. "I have nothing but admiration for airline pilots. They can't be paid enough as far as I'm concerned."

"That's what Carl always says," she replied. "He says you can fly for thirty years without incident, but when you do have a situation where everyone's life is on the line, you earn whatever you've been paid all those years, and more, to save lives."

"No argument from me," I said.

"Carl's my husband," she said brightly. Her name tag read BETSY SCHERER. I hadn't put her name and that of the pilot in the right-hand seat together until then.

"Oh, the first officer," I said. "What a nice young man. Are there many husbands and wives who work for the same airline?"

"Quite a few," she said, pulling out an empty coffeepot from her cart and replacing it with a full one. "It was nice that Mr. Silverton hired us together, sort of as a team."

"Very nice. Well, I'd better get back to my seat, and let you do your work uninterrupted."

"Enjoy the rest of your flight."

"I'm sure I will," I said.

Eventually, Captain Caine announced that we were beginning our descent into Stansted International Airport. I watched through the window as we broke through clouds and London's lights came to life below. The landing was so smooth that some passengers began applauding. As we taxied to our gate, Wayne Silverton came on the speaker.

"I trust you've enjoyed this first leg of the trip," he said, "but there is a lot more in store. We couldn't arrange to have everyone stay at the same hotel, but I'm sure you'll find all accommodations to be satisfactory. There will be a line of limousines waiting to take you into central London. For your information, there is good train service from Stansted into the city's Liverpool Street Station, but no need to be concerned about that. The hotel assigned to you is in your packet of printed material. Be sure and look for your hotel's name on signs the limo drivers will be holding. Any checked luggage will be delivered to your rooms. The hotels have been alerted that you'll probably be needing something to eat, and they've assured me that room service will be available. We will be meeting for breakfast at nine at the Savoy

Hotel. Until then, thanks for sharing this historic event with me, and for helping introduce America's new premium airline, SilverAir, to a discerning traveling public."

People applauded again and began to gather their belongings. I took advantage of the long taxi to the gate to go through the printed material we'd each received. Advance information sent to us in Cabot Cove said that our contingent would be staying at the Savoy, one of my favorite London hotels, and the material aboard confirmed it. The Silvertons, along with the cabin and flight deck crew, would also be staying there, and I was pleased to see that the crew wouldn't be relegated to spending the next two nights at a less opulent facility. Like any service business, SilverAir's success would depend upon the men and women who work for the company and who present its face to the public. Wayne was obviously aware of this and committed to keeping those frontline people happy, at least at this juncture.

As we proceeded down the aisle toward the exit door, I saw that only First Officer Scherer stood by the cockpit to greet deplaning passengers. Where was Captain Caine? I wondered. I peered into the cockpit; his seat was empty. I looked to my right and saw Ms. Molnari through a gap in the curtain that closed off the galley. I had only a fleeting glimpse of her, but she appeared to be crying.

After making our way through the airport, we stepped from the terminal into a damp, chilly night.

A heavy mist, almost rain, hung in the air. A fleet of limousines stood waiting, their engines running. Three drivers held large signs that read Savoy Hotel. Another lifted a sign indicating his vehicle was for the airline's crew. Seth, the Metzgers, and I greeted one of the Savoy drivers, whose vehicle was a stretch Mercedes limo that easily seated ten people. We climbed into the back.

"Pretty posh," Mort commented.

"Looks like Wayne is giving us the luxury treatment," I said.

"Seems like a waste of money to me," Seth growled. "Train would have been fine."

"Sit back and enjoy it, Doc," Mort said. "Like somebody once said, living well's the best revenge."

"Amen," Maureen said, obviously responding favorably to the pampering that came with the trip.

We were joined by others who'd be staying at the fabled Savoy, whose history and list of notable guests has no rival in London, or in most other major cities. The last one into the limousine was Christine Silverton, who slid in next to me on the rear bench seat.

The driver took off, rounding the corner of the terminal to take the road out of the airport.

"Oh, look," said Maureen.

I glanced over my shoulder to see a bank of spotlights trained on the fuselage of our plane, which was lit up like a Hollywood billboard. Christine didn't bother to turn around.

"Where's Wayne?" I asked, settling back beside her.

Her voice was flinty. "He has things to do here at the airport—he says!"

"There must be a never-ending list of things to do when starting up an airline," I said. "What a daunting undertaking."

She looked directly at me. Even in the dark car, I could see her eyes were moist from tears. "It isn't all him," she said in a hard voice, "although he may think it is."

I wondered if anyone else was listening to us, but the others seemed busy with their own conversations.

"Are you all right, Christine?" I asked.

"Oh, I am fine, Jessica, simply fine."

She turned away from me and I could hear, and feel, her heavy breathing, as though she was trying to bring in enough oxygen to inject some calm into her emotions. I considered pressing her but decided it was neither the time nor the place.

One thing was patently evident.

All might be well with SilverAir at thirty-five thousand feet.

But it wasn't so on the ground.

Chapter Three

The Savoy Hotel, located on the Strand on the bank of the Thames, has been a magnet for celebrities, heads of state, and other dignitaries since its construction in 1889 by an entrepreneur, Richard D'Oyly Carte, who'd originally discovered the works of Gilbert and Sullivan, and built the Savoy Theatre in which to present their operettas. He constructed the hotel next to the theater and followed his slogan, "Never compromise" to the extent that he hired César Ritz to manage it (Ritz eventually went off to create his own London landmark, The Ritz). Ritz, in turn, hired none other than the legendary Auguste Escoffier as chef. The standards were set high, and while the hotel fell into disrepair in the 1950s and 1960s, it's since been restored to its original stature and beyond. Although Johann Strauss no longer plays waltzes in the restaurant, and the magnificent voice of Caruso isn't heard there these days, the Savoy captures the hearts of everyone who stays there, including this lady. My late husband, Frank, and I spent our honeymoon there, and I've returned many times since when visiting London for pleasure or on business.

We were checked in and taken to our rooms. To my surprise, I'd been given one of the Edwardian riverside apartment suites, a favorite of visiting movie stars and other people of note. Noel Coward, Liza Minnelli, and Goldie Hawn are just a few of the hundreds of famous people, including kings and queens, who've basked in the luxury of the apartments, with their spectacular views of the Thames. The huge living room was filled with antiques and featured detailed plasterwork on the ceilings. The bed was king-sized and covered with fine Irish linen sheets; the spacious bathroom was a dazzling display of art deco marble and gleaming chrome fixtures.

I felt like a queen.

A tall vase holding a dozen long-stemmed red roses dominated a round table in the living room's center. I pulled the small card from where it had been pinned to the covering paper and opened it.

Welcome to London, dear Jessica. It will be wonderful seeing you again.

Love, George

The aroma of the roses was as pleasurable as the contemplation of seeing my dear friend George Sutherland. George is a senior Scotland Yard inspector whom I met years ago while in London as a guest of a mystery-writing colleague, Dame Marjorie Ainsworth. Marjorie was considered one of the world's greatest writers of crime novels, as the British prefer to call murder mysteries. She had invited me to her manor house outside of London when I was in England as a guest panelist at an international mystery conference. While I was there, she was brutally stabbed to death in her bed. First on the scene was George Sutherland, to whom I took an immediate liking, even though he viewed me as much of a suspect as others in the house that weekend. We ended up collaborating in solving Marjorie's murder and—well, I suppose you can say that we developed a keen interest in each other beyond simply having worked together. George is widowed, as am I, and although neither of us is impatient to develop another full-fledged romance, I must admit that George has championed that possibility at times, and the temptation has been strong for me, too. But we've agreed the prudent thing for us at this stage in our lives is to go slowly and see where things naturally evolve.

I'd called him prior to leaving Cabot Cove for the SilverAir inaugural flight and told him I'd be in London for only two days, and mentioned where I'd be staying. How sweet of him to have sent flowers. Among many wonderful attributes—he's a handsome gentleman with a Scottish brogue modified by years of living in London—is a sensitivity not always found in men who spend their adult lives investigating the darker side of the human condition.

I went to the window, parted the drapes, and looked down at the twinkling lights of boats on the Thames as they glided by. I suppose I was lost in a reverie of sorts because when the phone rang, it startled me to the extent that I flinched and knocked over the receiver as I reached for the phone.

"Jessica? Are you there?"

"Hello," I said, fumbling with the phone. "Yes. I—"

"I know I'm not waking you because I had the desk clerk at the hotel ring me when your party checked in."

"George!" I laughed, delighted to hear the voice of the man I'd just been thinking about. "How did you get him to do that?"

"You might say I pulled rank," he said, chuckling. "A nice young chap, very impressed that someone from the Yard called."

"The flowers are beautiful, George. Thank you."

"The least I could do. I realize you're probably exhausted from the trip and the time change, your circadian rhythms thoroughly turned upside down, so I won't keep you from getting some needed sleep. But tomorrow, I—"

"Actually, I'm wide-awake," I said, glancing at my watch. "It's only five o'clock back home."

"That's encouraging."

"It is?"

"Are you up for a nightcap?"

"I believe I am. Where are you?"

"Downstairs in the lobby."

"You're—?" I couldn't help but laugh. "You are more devious than you let on, George."

"We shan't make it a long drink, Jessica. The American Bar, say, in ten minutes?"

"Make it twenty minutes. I need to unpack and freshen up."

"Take all the time you need," he said. "I'll secure us a proper table."

George sprung to his feet as he saw me enter the Savoy's American Bar, which has its own history. Legend has it that it was where the martini was introduced, although that's subject to debate. Certainly, it was where the cocktail was popularized in London. It was bustling with people as we smiled at each other, closed the gap, and embraced. Once seated, George said, "You look absolutely splendid, Jessica. Obviously, the long flight didn't take its toll on you."

"Don't be so sure," I said, waving away his compliment. "I suspect that in a half hour I'll be ready to fall on my nose."

"We can't have that," he said. "Much too pretty a nose to have that happen."

"You look wonderful, George," I said, "very relaxed and at peace with the world."

He wore what could almost be considered a uniform for him: a blue button-down shirt, a Harris tweed jacket, a muted tie, tan slacks with a razor crease, and ankle-high boots shined to a mirror finish. A little gray had crept into his hairline, but not much. It was his eyes that always drew me, probably because they seemed fascinated by everything and everyone, soft eyes the color of Granny Smith apples, but eyes that never missed a thing.

"Thank you, Jessica. What will you have to drink?"

"A glass of sherry would be nice," I said. George had what he almost always orders, a single-malt scotch.

Drinks in hand, we toasted to being together again.

"So," I said, "tell me what sensational crimes you've been solving since the last time I saw you."

"Afraid there's not much to report," he said. "The usual, angry or unhappy spouses killing their better halves—I will never understand why they don't simply walk away rather than taking a life. But that's for the sociologists to answer, I suppose, and they don't seem to have a clue. You, Jessica? Working on a new book?"

"Not at the moment, although I am putting together a plot for the next one. I'm enjoying not being tied to my computer and having to produce pages. That's why I agreed to come on the first flight of SilverAir."

"How was it?"

"Very nice. The airline's founder, Wayne Silverton, grew up in Cabot Cove."

"I know."

"Do you?"

"When you told me about your invitation, I did a little checking into the airline. It's gotten quite a bit of press here in the UK."

"I imagine it would since London is one of its original destinations. What does the press have to say?"

"Mostly mixed. Some of our travel writers and editors applaud Mr. Silverton's courage in starting an airline in the midst of so many airline bankruptcies, and think providing more comfortable surroundings is good for the traveling public. Others? There are detractors."

"Who consider it foolhardy?"

"Not exactly. A few business writers have delved into Mr. Silverton's financing for the airline. They aren't terribly impressed with those he's chosen to partner with, including some chaps here in the UK, one of whom has a rather unsavory reputation."

"Oh? I met one of Wayne Silverton's partners on the flight, a Mr. Casale."

"Ah, yes. His name has come up, too."

"It sounds as though you've done more than just a little checking into the airline."

"In the genes, I suppose. There's been considerable interest in how your Mr. Silverton and his airline managed to circumvent the usual means of gaining approval to use Stansted Airport. It seems they hired some very well-connected lobbyists here in the UK who—how shall I say it?—greased the skids for their client."

"Greased the skids, as in bought access?" I asked.

"Exactly. Who paid that money, and more important, who received it in the Civil Aviation Authority, is still closely guarded information. I should hasten to mention that this is all alleged. What we do know for a fact is that SilverAir gained access to gates at Stansted far faster than any other airline looking for accommodation there."

I sat back, processed what he'd said, and sipped my sherry. "You said the name Casale came up, too, George. In what context?"

He smiled and came forward in his chair, leatherpatched elbows on the table. "I hope I'm not sounding like some naysayer," he said, "dragging up for you only the bad news about your friend's partners in his airline. There's millions of dollars invested in it from reputable banks here in London and New York."

"I'm not taking it wrong, George. I'm naturally interested. Please go on."

He sat back again and rubbed his chin. "Well," he said, "Mr. Casale—I believe his first name is Salvatore—Mr. Casale is reputed to have very solid connections with the Mafia in the States. Las Vegas casinos."

"Wayne Silverton told me that he and Mr. Casale were involved in some real estate business in Las Vegas."

"Not surprising. Of course, we have our own shadowy investor here in the UK, Churlson Vicks."

"Interesting first name," I said.

"Family name of some sort, I suppose. At any rate,

Vicks has made his millions compliments of our government, and other governments around the world. He seems to have a knack for bidding high and getting the jobs because no one else is invited to bid against him. A bit like your Halliburton. Vicks is also rumored to deal in illegal military arms to third world countries and provide needed medicines to poorer nations at outrageous markups, all alleged but never formally charged. Nothing like having friends in high places."

"And money," I said.

"Yes, it's always the money, isn't it?"

"Except in murder."

"You mean money is just one of the motivations for murder," he said.

"There's also revenge, jealousy, fear, a whole range of emotions."

"Of course," he said. "But we're not talking about murder here, are we?"

"No, and I hope it stays that way. I've had my fill of being in the wrong place at the wrong time when murders take place."

"Yes, you have had your share of such unfortunate events," he said. "More sherry?"

"Thank you, no," I said.

"You're here in London for only two nights?"

I nodded.

He took my hand. "I hope this drink doesn't constitute all we'll see of each other."

I sighed and shook my head. "It might be, George.

I don't know what plans have been made, although I assume Wayne has come up with something to entertain us. We're all expected to meet for breakfast here at the Savoy, but I'll make time for us. Maybe lunch tomorrow or, even better, dinner. What's your schedule?"

"Relatively free. I'm off the clock unless something unusual pops up."

I heard a buzz and George grimaced.

"Sorry," he said, releasing my hand and flipping open his cell phone. "Sutherland here." He pulled a small notepad from the inside pocket of his jacket and made notes as he listened. "Yes, I see. You're certain of the victim's identity?" He made a few more notes. "Yes, I'll go there immediately." He snapped shut the cover on his phone.

"I have a feeling that something unusual has popped up," I said with a gentle laugh.

"The older I get," he said, "the more I believe in and respect coincidences." He took my hand in both of his.

I cocked my head.

"There's been a murder at Stansted Airport."

My eyes widened. "Yes," I said, "that is a coincidence."

"More than you think, Jessica. I'm terribly sorry to tell you that the victim, according to what I've just been told, is your friend Mr. Wayne Silverton."

Chapter Four

One of the Savoy's valet attendants held open the door of George's silver Jaguar for me. George helped me into the left-hand seat and went around to the right where he slipped behind the wheel. This was, after all, the United Kingdom, where people drive on the "wrong" side of the road. Or, as the British prefer, drive on the "other side."

"I don't know any more than what I've already told you," George said, looking over to assure that I was belted in before fastening his own seat belt. "Our desk officer said that local bobbies are securing the area. Family hasn't been notified yet."

"But he was certain of the name of the victim?"

He nodded sharply as he steered the car out of the Savoy's drive and into London traffic. It was late, but it could have been midday, judging from the multitude of cars crowding the street and the number of pedestrians strolling the sidewalks. George glanced at his watch. "Theaters are getting out," he said. "It'll be slow going escaping town."

I sat quietly while he concentrated on which roads would allow him to evade the worst of the traffic. My thoughts were riveted on our destination and what awaited us.

How ironic that on the night of his triumph, the debut of his new airline, Wayne Silverton should be murdered. And by whom? Whom had he offended so egregiously that the only solution was murder? He had a quick temper; I was witness to that in his exchange with Captain Caine over the aircraft's technical problem. George had suggested that Wayne's business connections were skirting the edge of respectability. The reporters on the plane had hinted of "connections." Had one of his partners in this venture, or perhaps in his Las Vegas dealings, become dissatisfied with their business arrangement? What could have been the "things he had to do" that his wife said were keeping him at the airport? If he had accompanied her and the rest of his guests to the hotel, would he still be alive? Who else from our group may have lingered at Stansted? Was it possible that Wayne had been killed by someone who'd been on the flight? Maybe it was a worker at the airport. My mind was awhirl with these and other questions without any answers—at least for the moment. All I knew was what George had told me, that Wayne's death had been reported.

I straightened in my seat.

"Something occur to you, Jessica?" George asked as we reached the entrance to a highway and pulled onto it. The sign said it was the A11.

"I was just thinking that for people like Wayne Silverton, the road to success is often strewn with enemies."

"The price you pay, I suppose," he said, accelerating, the Jaguar's engine a faint, smooth whine as it propelled us along, passing every car on the road.

"I was also thinking how ironic my words were back at the bar, that I was happy not to be in the wrong place at the wrong time when murder takes place."

He glanced at me. "Perhaps you shouldn't have come with me," he said.

"Oh, no," I said. "How could I *not* come? Only a few hours ago I was happily winging along at thirty-five thousand feet in a lovely, spacious, modern jet aircraft, feasting on caviar and shrimp and chateaubriand, and reading a good book. And now—"

"And now your host has been murdered. Hang on."

He made a sudden, sharp move that sent us hurtling between two huge trucks as though we'd been slung from a slingshot. He immediately shifted to the left lane and exited onto another highway, the A118.

"Sorry," he said, sensing my discomfort.

"You're a very confident driver, George," I said, hoping the lump in my throat wasn't too evident.

We eventually took a third highway—the A406 I think it was—until reaching the entrance to Stansted International Airport.

"Know where your aircraft was parked?" he asked.

"Down that way, I think," I said, referring to the last terminal in a row of four.

As we approached, SilverAir's 767 came into view. It was still bathed in spotlights; Wayne had said that he wanted the plane illuminated at night wherever and whenever it was parked. Seeing the tail jutting into the night sky, its emblem gleaming proudly in the intense light, was unsettling, considering what had occurred.

As we pulled up in front of the terminal, it was obvious that something unusual had happened inside. A cadre of uniformed police stood guard at the main doors. An array of marked police vehicles choked the area, lights flashing from their roofs and casting a macabre aura over the scene, as though it was a theatrical production.

We got out of the car, and I followed George as he went up to one of the officers and showed his identification. The bobbie stiffened, hit a military brace, and told George to follow him inside. He saw me fall into line, stopped, and asked who I was.

"She's with me," George said.

"Yes, sir."

We followed the young officer the length of the main corridor off which numbered gates were located, some with lounges filled with passengers awaiting their flights, others void of people. We eventually arrived at the gate, which I recognized as the one into which we'd deplaned earlier in the evening. It was cordoned off with crime scene tape, and a dozen officers, both uniformed and plainclothed, milled about. George again showed his ID, and we were allowed to enter the lounge and go to the Jetway leading to the aircraft. I hung back as George conferred with a man wearing a tan raincoat, obviously someone senior. George turned to me. "He's inside, in the cockpit," he said. "Want to wait out here?"

I silently debated for a few seconds before saying, "No, I'd like to come with you."

We walked down the Jetway to the aircraft's main door where still another officer stood. George indicated for me to wait. I watched as he moved past the officer and disappeared into the flight deck. My wait for him to emerge seemed endless, although it must have been no more than a few minutes. He poked his head out and motioned for me to join him. Up until that moment, I'd been eager to accompany him into the cockpit, but I was now hesitant. His raised eyebrows said, "Either come or stay, Jessica. Don't prolong this."

I joined him at the cockpit door and looked inside. The lighting was dim and diffused. But even in the shadowy illumination I saw the figure of a person in the left-hand seat usually occupied by the aircraft's captain. Obviously, the body was that of Wayne Silverton, although I couldn't see his face. George took a few steps into the area, and I followed. Now, the scene was clearer, and tragically real. Silverton's lifeless form was slumped forward over the pilot's control yoke, his weight pushing it fully forward. His head was turned to the right, his mouth open as though he was about to say something. His eyes were open, too. Had he seen the person who'd shoved the knife into his upper back? His eyes were clear, indicating he'd died less than eight hours ago. After about eight hours, the deceased's eyes take on a cloudy, milky appearance. Of course, we also knew from the timeline that he'd been murdered more recently than that.

The knife's handle was black, as was its quillon, or hilt, the piece separating the handle from the blade, creating what looked like a small cross projecting upward from just below his neck. Blood had seeped from the wound through his white dress shirt; his suit jacket lay crumpled on the right-hand seat. His right hand rested on the thrust levers, which, when pushed forward, provided power to the jet engines, a plane's equivalent of an automobile's accelerator.

I leaned forward to get a closer look at the weapon that had been used to kill him. Judging from the length of the handle, it was not a large knife. On even closer examination it appeared to be a switchblade, with a slot in the handle into which the blade could be folded. I also observed that whoever wielded the weapon had used considerable force. The hilt was pressed into the shirt's fabric and the flesh beneath it.

I stepped back to allow George to get closer. He placed his fingertips on the side of Wayne's neck, then the palm of his hand. "Still warm," he muttered. "He hasn't been dead long."

A commotion from outside the flight deck caused us to turn. A coroner had arrived, along with two medical technicians in white lab coats.

"Let's give them room to work," George said, and led me out into the passenger cabin. There was something surreal about the plane's interior at that moment, all the empty seats that had so recently been filled with happy men and women having a good time while crossing the Atlantic as invited guests of SilverAir. I saw in my imagination people in those seats and wondered whether one of them had jammed the knife into our host. Hopefully—and it was the wildest of hopes—he'd been murdered not by one of his guests, but by a deranged stranger who'd come upon him sitting in the cockpit.

Why was he sitting in the cockpit?

"Why was he sitting in the cockpit?" I asked George.

"Good question," he said as we made our way back down the Jetway to the departure and arrival lounge.

"Do you think he might have been moved there?" I asked.

"No," George said. "There would have been signs of it. I saw none."

He was right. I, too, had looked for traces of Wayne having been dragged onto the flight deck. There weren't any, but I thought I'd ask anyway. I'd learned years ago that it was always wise to seek an opinion that might run counter to what you'd decided.

The officer in the tan raincoat approached us. "Got a minute, Inspector?" he asked.

"Excuse me," George said to me and walked to a relatively secluded corner of the lounge where a middle-aged man wearing the uniform of a private security guard stood with two officers. After they'd been introduced, they took seats on a bench. George took out a notebook and began writing as the security guard spoke animatedly.

I walked from the lounge into the wide hallway that linked the terminal's gates, and watched people come and go. Many were obviously aware that something untoward had taken place—the number of uniformed officers and the crime scene tape saw to that—and congregated as close as they dared in the hope of learning more. I kept one eye on George and the man he was interviewing while taking in others. Eventually, George and the man stood and shook hands. I started back, but just before I entered the lounge, I spotted a familiar face, Captain Bill Caine, who stood at the fringe of the crowd. I raised my hand and made a move toward him, but he turned and was lost in the crowd. I tried to go after him, but the people closed ranks and I couldn't see him over the heads of the others.

Strange, I thought.

"You all right, Jessica?" George said, coming up behind me.

"I just saw the captain of our flight," I told him.

"Oh?" George said flatly, reviewing some notes he had written.

"Yes. I wonder why he's here at the airport," I said.

George shrugged. "Seems a logical place for an airline pilot to be."

"Yes, of course," I said, "but I assumed he'd gone into London with the rest of us. He and Wayne Silverton had argued during the flight."

This time his "Oh?" was delivered with more interest. "Tell me about it," he said.

I recounted the confrontation between Silverton and Caine over the malfunctioning light on the control panel.

"I'll ask Captain Caine about it. He's on my list of those to interview," George said. "By the way, I was in communication with my superiors at the Yard. It seems they've decided that I'm to stay on this case as lead investigator."

My immediate, unspoken reaction was pleasure at the news. Whether George was pleased was another matter.

"You know what that means?" he said. "You may have another passenger on the flight home."

"You?"

He nodded. "My superiors think it might prove worthwhile for me to accompany those who were on the flight, get to know them better, perhaps well enough to identify the murderer."

"I, ah—"

He smiled and touched my arm. "Hardly a conventional reason for us to spend time together, Jessica, but I'll take it."

Cupid is a murderer, I thought.

"Besides," he said, "I'll need your help. You have better instincts and observational skills than most professional detectives I've worked with."

"That's flattering," I said, "but if it's all the same to you, I'd just as soon leave it to professionals—like you."

He looked at me and smiled, and I had to smile, too. We both knew that my natural curiosity gene had already kicked in, and that it would be impossible for me to remain uninvolved.

"I have to get back to headquarters," he said.

"Of course. May I ride back with you, or would you rather I find other transportation?"

"No, you're coming with me. I'll drop you at the hotel. I'm afraid I've been assigned to break the news to the victim's wife. You know her?"

"Yes, but not well. Her name is Christine. She's

a former airline stewardess—back when they were called that."

"Would you consider—?" He stopped, as if weighing his request.

"Being with you when you tell her? Of course."

"Thank you."

We remained at the airport for another fifteen minutes while George issued a final set of orders. A uniformed officer who'd been standing guard over George's Jaguar opened the door for me, and with George behind the wheel we headed back to London. He drove more slowly than he had on the way to Stansted, which caused me less anxiety. But while the pace might have been slower, my brain was racing.

"Who was the man you interviewed?" I asked after we'd turned onto the A406.

"An airport security guard assigned to the SilverAir plane. I have the feeling that he wasn't especially diligent, although he did have something of interest to offer."

"What was that?"

"He said he was there when Mr. Silverton entered the plane."

"That could be helpful," I said, "to establish the time sequence."

"Right you are. But I was more interested in what else he saw. He claims to have seen someone follow Silverton aboard."

I stiffened. "Who was it?" I asked.

"I'm afraid he wasn't much help there. He says

he'd gone to get a cup of tea from a vendor and was on his way back when this second person got on."

"No one was on duty while he went for his tea?" I asked.

"He claims he never took his eyes off the plane because the vendor wasn't far away. I doubt that, but I didn't challenge him. The important thing is that he did see a second person."

"A man?"

"Or a woman."

"He doesn't know?"

"Unfortunately, no. All he saw, he said, was a person wearing a dark coat of some type."

"He didn't board to see who it was?"

George laughed. "You ask the same questions I asked," he said. "No, he did not. He says he didn't want to intrude on Silverton. He's well aware that Silverton owns—or owned—the airline."

"A shame he didn't follow up. He didn't see this second person leave?"

"Not according to him. Of course, he assured me that he never left his post again, except—"

"There was an exception?"

"Nature called, he said. Tea will sometimes do that to you, especially a large take-out container."

My sigh was long and loud.

"So much for security," George said. "Tell me again about this argument between Silverton and the captain. Blaine, was it?"

"Caine," I corrected, and told him again what I remembered of the flight deck dispute.

"Doesn't sound like much of a flap, but I'll raise it when I have a word with him," George said.

"I think we—you—should check taxi services to see who might have taken a fare earlier in the evening to Stansted Airport."

"Good suggestion, Jessica. As far as you know, were any of your fellow passengers intending to extend their stay in London beyond the return flight?"

I shook my head. "I don't know."

We said little else for the rest of the trip. My thoughts were focused on the unpleasant task of telling Christine Silverton of her husband's murder. I also pondered whether to wake Seth, Mort, Maureen, and the Shevlins to give them the news. I decided against it. The news would be broken to everyone at breakfast the following morning.

As we got out of the Jaguar and walked into the lobby, I realized that of everyone at breakfast, there might be one person for whom the news wouldn't come as a shock.

Whoever murdered Wayne Silverton would already know.

Chapter Five

It became immediately apparent as we crossed the lobby that the news wouldn't have to wait until breakfast. It seemed that half of my fellow passengers were there. Upon spotting me come through the door, Seth Hazlitt, Mort and Maureen Metzger, and Mayor Shevlin jumped up from couches and surrounded George and me.

"And where have you been?" Seth asked sternly.

"I was—"

"We've been worried sick about you," said Maureen.

"I've been with George. You've met Inspector Sutherland."

"*Ayuh*," Seth said, accepting George's outstretched hand. "Good evening, Inspector."

"Good evening, Doctor," George said.

The others greeted George, too. They'd met when he visited Cabot Cove, and he and Seth had spent time together when the three of us were in Washington, D.C. I was aware that Seth wasn't particularly fond of George, the reason pure speculation. Because of my close friendship with Seth for so many years, and the fact that we were both single, there had been occasional conjecture that he and I were linked romantically. That wasn't true, but rumors like that are hard to dispel. What was behind Seth's discomfort with my closeness with George was, I felt, perhaps the protective instincts longtime friends have for each other. Seth and I weren't far apart in age, but he tended to assume a paternal stance with me, like a father concerned that his daughter might choose the wrong man. It was all silly, I know, and totally unnecessary, but that was Seth. On the one hand, I loved him for it. He obviously had my best interests at heart. On the other hand, I did find myself occasionally irked at being treated like a flibbertigibbet incapable of making sound adult decisions. I suppose I had given him cause at times through sticky situations in which I'd found myself, particularly when they involved danger. And here I was again in close proximity to a murder, the stickiest of all possible situations.

"Is it true?" Maureen asked. "Wayne is dead?"

"I'm afraid so," I said. "How did you know?"

"There was a reporter here asking questions."

"Then does Christine know?" I asked.

They looked at each other before Jim Shevlin said, "I haven't seen her. Have you, Mort?"

"No," Mort answered.

"She's got to be told," I said. "George and I came to break the news to her."

George said, "It would be good if Dr. Hazlitt would accompany us. Having a physician on hand might be prudent."

"I'm willing," Seth said.

By now, the circle of people surrounding us had grown to a few dozen, including one of the reporters on the trip. A flurry of questions erupted asking for details of what had happened at Stansted, none of which, I knew, George would be willing to answer.

"I'll ring Christine's room," I said, and walked toward a bank of house phones. George and Seth followed, the lingering questions fading behind us. I picked up the phone and asked for Mrs. Silverton's suite.

"I'm afraid we don't put through calls to guest rooms at this hour," the operator said, "unless there's been prior approval."

"This is an emergency," I said. "Mrs. Silverton will want to receive my call. I'm Jessica Fletcher, another guest at the hotel."

"I appreciate that, ma'am, but—"

George gently took the phone from me. "This is Scotland Yard Inspector George Sutherland," he said in a calm, yet firm voice. "This call to Mrs. Silverton is official police business."

"Yes, sir."

George handed me the phone as Christine picked up.

"Christine," I said, "it's Jessica Fletcher. I'm sorry to be calling so late but—"

"You're not waking me," she said. "What is it?"

"We . . . need to talk with you. May I come up to your room?" I said. "Seth Hazlitt is with me, and another man, George Sutherland."

"What is it?" she asked. "Is something wrong?"

"May we come up?" I said.

"Yes, of course."

We rode the elevator to her floor, found the suite, and I knocked. Christine opened the door immediately. She covered her mouth with her hand and retreated into the suite's recesses. "Something's happened to Wayne, hasn't it?" she said without turning to face us.

"Yes, ma'am," George said. "I'm Inspector Sutherland, Scotland Yard. I'm terribly sorry to be the bearer of bad news. I'm afraid your husband has been found dead at Stansted Airport."

She remained with her back to us. There was a discernible heaving of her shoulders, and then the sound of gentle sobs. I placed my hands on her upper arms and asked, "Would you like to sit, Christine?"

She didn't reply, simply pulled away from me and went to a small swivel club chair covered in a floral print on which she'd flung her navy blue raincoat. She dropped it to the floor. I picked it up. It felt damp. I took it to the closet and reached in to remove a hanger. The closet was empty except for unused hangers. I hung the coat and turned back to the room where I noticed that four suitcases stood unopened on folding racks.

"How?" Christine asked no one in particular. "What happened? A heart attack? An accident?"

"Your husband was murdered," George said.

"Murdered?" she said, her face angry. "That's absurd. There must be a mistake."

"Afraid not, Christine," said Seth.

"Do you think you could answer a few questions, Mrs. Silverton?" George asked.

Christine popped up out of her chair. "Questions? At this time? Of course not," she said pacing back and forth.

"We'll make it tomorrow, then," George said.

"But *I* have questions," she said, her voice rising to a shriek.

"Maybe tomorrow would be a better time for them, too," Seth suggested.

Christine stopped pacing, eyes narrowed, lips a slash across her pretty face. "How was he killed?" she demanded.

George looked at me and Seth before answering. "He was stabbed," he said.

"Where?"

"In his back."

"I don't mean that," she snapped. "Where did it happen?"

"On the flight deck of the aircraft that brought us here," I said. "He was found in the captain's seat."

Her laugh was sardonic. "Good God," she said. "Wayne was always a frustrated airline pilot. He loved to sneak into the cockpit of one of our SilverAir planes when no one else was around and pretend he was flying it. It was all fantasy with him. The whole thing was a fantasy. Owning an airline was a fantasy."

That knife sticking out of his back was no fantasy, I thought. But of course, I didn't express it.

"Would you like me to prescribe something for you, Christine?" Seth asked. "Something to help you sleep, perhaps."

"No, I'm all right," she said. "I don't want to sleep."

"Would you prefer to be alone?" Seth asked.

She nodded.

"I'll stay a few minutes," I said, my expression indicating that I thought Seth and George should leave.

"I'd best go now," George said. "They're expecting me at headquarters. A word, Jessica?"

"I'll be right back," I told Christine, and accompanied the men into the hallway, using my foot to keep the door ajar.

"I think it's a good idea for you to stay with her," Seth said in a low voice, "at least for a while. I'll be in my room if she changes her mind, or if you need anything."

"Good," I said. To George: "When will I see you again?"

"In the morning. You say there's a breakfast planned?"

"At nine. That's what the schedule says."

"I'll be here earlier than that."

"Call me when you arrive."

"She appears to be all right at the moment," Seth said, "but the shock really hasn't hit home. Keep an eye on her, Jessica."

I assured him I would, said good night, and watched them walk down the hall and disappear into a waiting elevator. When I returned to the room, Christine was standing at the window.

"Would you like me to order something up from room service?" I asked softly so as not to startle her.

She turned. "Thank you, Jessica. Yes, I would like something. I haven't eaten."

"We had quite a big meal on the flight," I said as I sat at a desk and found the room service menu. "Something simple?"

"Just tea," she said. "Maybe some toast, or a scone."

I placed the order. Christine sat on the couch, her long legs crossed, her foot bouncing up and down. She wore the same stylish, tailored blue pantsuit she had during the flight.

"How did you happen to go to the airport, Jessica?" she asked.

"I was having a drink downstairs in the American Bar with Inspector Sutherland—he's an old friend I haven't seen in a while—when he received a call that there had been a murder at the airport. I went with him."

"You saw Wayne?"

"Yes."

"I'm surprised that someone like you, a civilian, was allowed such access," she said.

"As I said, I was with the inspector. Christine, do you have any idea who might have wanted to kill Wayne?"

"Would you like a list?" she replied. "I can write one out for you."

I said nothing.

"Surprised?" she said.

"Yes," I said. "You're saying he had many enemies?"

"Many, and if you're compiling a list of suspects, include me on it."

My initial reaction was to call Seth and have him come to the suite. Had the shock now worn off and she was about to have a breakdown?

"Don't take me literally," she said. "I didn't really want Wayne dead, although there have been times when the thought was appealing."

"I thought—I assumed you and Wayne were happy together," I said. "You have so much in common with your aviation backgrounds, and now this exciting new venture."

"Unfortunately, Wayne's 'aviation background' includes too much time spent with attractive flight attendants."

I thought of the ravishing Gina Molnari.

Christine slowly shook her head. "Remember the book back in the sixties, *Coffee, Tea or Me?*" she asked.

"Of course," I said. "I read it like millions of others did. It was—funny."

"Those were the high-flying days of air travel, Jessica. It was so glamorous back then to be a stewardess, winging around the globe with planes full of happy, successful people, everyone in a good mood, the service wonderful, the crews tight-knit. We were all one big happy family. Of course, that book played up the sexual exploits of stewardesses."

"Yes, I recall that, although it was tame by today's standards."

"I suppose it was. Wayne was very much a part of that era."

"But that was then," I said, "before he met you."

"He didn't change, Jessica. There was always another woman in the wings, always someone younger and more beautiful. I'm sure you've noticed what an attractive man Wayne is. Or was."

I was gripped with mixed emotions. If venting this way would help her overcome the shock of learning that her husband had been murdered, I was willing to be a sounding board. At the same time, I was growing increasingly uncomfortable being privy to such intimate thoughts from a woman whom I knew, but not well.

"I shouldn't be going on like this," she said, and

forced a laugh. "If being married to a philandering husband is motive for murder, you can put me at the top of your list." She stood. "I appreciate you being here, Jessica, but I'm suddenly exhausted. And I need to make some phone calls before I go to bed. I'm sure tomorrow will be anything but pleasant."

"Of course," I said as someone knocked on the door. "Must be room service."

"Tell them to go away," Christine said. "Have it delivered to your room."

"All right," I said. "You're sure there's nothing I can do, nothing I can get you?"

"Positive. Thanks. Good night."

I stepped into the hallway where a bellman in a starched white jacket stood by an elaborately set rolling service cart. "Sorry," I said, "but there's been a change. You can bring this to my room."

Chapter Six

Although I was exhausted from the long day and the events of the past few hours, sleep was out of the question. I nibbled on a scone and sipped some tea, but food wasn't on my mind at the moment. I suppose the shock of Wayne Silverton's murder had now fully settled in with me, as I'm sure it had with Christine Silverton.

I'd found her reaction to be somewhat strange, but that wasn't fair. Prosecutors in murder trials often try to find something nefarious in how a defendant reacts to the news of a loved one's murder. But psychologists know that each individual projects a different emotional state when hit with such devastating news. There are those who remain stoic and pragmatic, while others fall apart. To assume that the stoic, pragmatic mourner must be guilty because of the lack of emotion is to come to a tenuous conclusion.

I changed into my nightclothes and a comfortable

robe provided by the hotel, sat by the window, and tried to make sense out of what few facts had emerged since I learned of Wayne's death.

He'd been stabbed in the cockpit of the 767, and was there, according to Christine, because he enjoyed fantasizing about being a commercial airline pilot. How many other people besides Christine knew of this harmless bit of playacting? Whoever had killed Wayne was aware of where he was, or would be, at that particular moment.

Obviously, the airline captain, Bill Caine, had not gone into London with the rest of the crew. He'd argued with Wayne during the flight. I'd seen him at the airport while there with George Sutherland. There was nothing unusual about that, except that when he saw me, he rushed away. Surely, he recognized me. Why hadn't he approached and asked what I knew about the scene taking place at the departure and arrival lounge? Why had he disappeared so quickly?

Christine's admission that her husband was a womanizer was off-putting. I'd been uncomfortable being on the receiving end of her sad confession, and felt deeply for her—if what she said was true. If it was, she had every reason to be angry with Wayne. Angry enough to kill him? It appeared to me that she hadn't stayed in her room at the Savoy once we arrived. Her coat was damp, and she hadn't bothered to unpack the suitcases. She'd had enough time to go back to Stansted and return to the hotel before we arrived at her suite. I realized I was viewing her as a suspect in her husband's murder, which was perhaps premature. But how could I not wonder who was the murderer amongst us?

Wayne's business partners in SilverAir? The Brit, Churlson Vicks, with his unsavory reputation? Mr. Casale, Wayne's former real estate partner in Las Vegas? He hadn't sounded especially enamored of being a partner in an airline.

I decided that the best thing I could do at that juncture was to put these thoughts, along with dozens of others, out of my mind and get some sleep. But I had to laugh as I attempted to force that to happen. As a psychiatrist friend of mine says, tell someone not to think of purple elephants and that's all they'll think of. I finally dozed off, thinking that given a choice between purple elephants and murder, I'd settle for colorful pachyderms every time.

Chapter Seven

After a few hours of fitful sleep, I was up, showered, and dressed by six. I went downstairs where it looked like a number of my travel companions had also found sleep to be difficult. They milled about the lobby, some with coffee or tea they'd brought from their rooms, others sitting quietly with blank expressions on their faces. I joined Seth Hazlitt and the Metzgers.

"Doc told me about breaking the news to Mrs. Silverton," Mort said. "I don't envy you that job. It's the one I always dread the most."

"She took it quite well," Seth said. "Jessica stayed with her after the inspector and I left. How did she hold up, Jessica?"

"Relatively well. Naturally, she was shaken and eventually wanted to be alone."

We all turned at the arrival of a camera and sound-man and a reporter from a TV station. They were followed by a man and a woman who had the hungry look of reporters from a different medium, probably print. The man had an expensive digital camera hanging from his neck. They came directly to me.

"You're Jessica Fletcher, the crime writer," the female reporter said without hesitation.

"Yes."

She introduced herself as being from a notorious London tabloid. While she did, her photographer sidekick took a succession of photos of me and everyone nearby.

"I wish you wouldn't do that," I said to the photographer, who'd inched toward me and had the lens of his camera only a few feet from my face.

He moved even closer.

I turned away.

Mort intervened, stepping between me and the photographer. "The lady doesn't want her picture taken," he said.

"Who are you?" asked the reporter.

"Morton Metzger, sheriff of Cabot Cove, Maine."

The man and woman looked at each other and shrugged.

"Come on, Mrs. F.," Mort said, leading me away from the pair. "Couple 'a ghouls."

"Maybe we should go into the dining room," I suggested.

"Breakfast is in one of their private rooms," Mort said. "The hotel changed it because of what happened last night, to give us some privacy."

"Good thinking," Seth said, following Mort, Maureen, and me toward the dining room entrance.

Followed by a young man and woman George Sutherland came through the front door. As they approached us, the photographer shot more pictures.

"I see you're already up and around," George said to me, leaving his assistants to wave away the press.

"I couldn't sleep," I said.

"I don't wonder." He said hello to the others and introduced his colleagues as part of his special investigative unit at Scotland Yard. He took me aside. "I suggested to the management that you have your breakfast in a private room," he said.

"I thought you might have been behind the change," I said. "Thank you."

"It will give me the opportunity to speak with the group en masse. Anything new since I left last night?"

"No. I stayed for a while with Mrs. Silverton."

"And?"

"She had some interesting things to say, but I'd rather wait to tell you until we have some time alone."

"Fair enough. I've received a passenger manifest from the airline with the names of those who traveled with you, as well as the crew. I'll want to do a head count once we've gathered."

One of the Savoy's executives came to the dining room entrance to announce that our private room was now open. "We'll be serving breakfast a little earlier than originally planned," he said. "I trust this won't be an inconvenience."

We filed into a large, ornate room in which tables had been set with white linens, crystal, and gleaming silverware. A lavish, colorful floral arrangement brightened the center of each table. Four young waiters and waitresses in uniform stood at the room's perimeter waiting for us to be seated so they could start serving.

The Cabot Cove group gathered at one of the tables. George asked me to save him a seat, which I did by placing my cardigan over the back of a chair.

As the room filled, there was the expected buzz about the murder. A lot of attention was directed at me once word got around that I'd been to Stansted Airport with the Scotland Yard inspector assigned to the case. I also caught a snippet of one conversation that questioned my relationship with that inspector, allowing me access to the crime scene.

George and his two fresh-faced young assistants stood in a corner discussing papers George was holding. A few people got up from their tables and approached him with questions, but he politely waved them off, always with a smile. But I knew that behind his ready, appealing grin were a steely backbone and razor-sharp intellect, both of which could be brought into play on a moment's notice.

I took note of who'd arrived, and more important, who hadn't. Christine Silverton wasn't there, which was understandable. She'd probably decided to order room service and avoid the pain of the condolences, and questions she'd undoubtedly have to endure.

The waitstaff served juices and coffee or tea. It was still earlier than breakfast had originally been planned for, and it appeared that they were expecting more guests to arrive. Finally, at eight thirty, Sal Casale rose from where he was seated with a gentleman I didn't recognize and asked for everyone's attention. Once he had it, he said, "As you all know, being here this morning isn't the way it was supposed to be. In case anyone hasn't heard, Wayne Silverton was found stabbed to death last night at the airport."

Even though Wayne's death wasn't news to anyone in the room, there were gasps and groans.

Casale held up his hand. "I'm not sure what this means for how we'll be spending the rest of our time in London, but that's being figured out now. In the meantime, I'd like to introduce you to our British partner, Mr. Churlson Vicks."

Vicks got to his feet, cleared his throat, and tapped his fist to his lips a few times. He was a solidly built gentleman wearing a gray suit with a muted stripe, a blue shirt with a white collar, and a burgundy tie. Everything about him was square: his jaw, forehead, and shoulders. I judged him to be in his early sixties, perhaps a few years younger. He looked every bit the successful businessman, his face unnaturally tanned, especially for one of British descent, his teeth whiter than they should have been for a man his age.

"We're all terribly shocked and upset over Wayne's brutal death," he said in a well-modulated voice tinged with a British accent. "Wayne was a visionary whose belief in a new era of air travel will be sorely missed." Another throat clearing and more taps to the mouth. "I believe that those who knew Wayne will agree that he would want us to forge ahead despite his demise, both with SilverAir, and with our plans for this inaugural trip to London. Therefore, the schedule you've been given will remain basically the same—except, of course, if the authorities charged with bringing Wayne's killer to justice have needs that necessitate change. Let me now introduce Inspector George Sutherland from our esteemed Scotland Yard."

George thanked Vicks, introduced his two associates, and said, "While I appreciate the reason you are here in London, and that a schedule has been established for you, I am afraid the investigation into Mr. Silverton's murder must take precedence. However, I will try not to inconvenience you too much. Since we are gathered together in this room, my associate, Ms. Simmons, will read names from the passenger and crew manifests provided by SilverAir's London operations office. Please respond when your name is called."

The young woman read off the names, eliciting a variety of responses—"Yo," "Here," "Present." When she was finished, she told George that there were eleven people who hadn't responded. I'd kept track as she read. Captain Caine and the flight attendant, Ms. Molnari, were among the missing, along with

Christine Silverton, and others whose names I didn't recognize.

"Thank you for indulging us in that exercise," George said. "Reminds one of being back in school, doesn't it?'

There were a few laughs.

"I will want to speak with each of you individually," he said. "Perhaps we'll have an opportunity to do that as the day progresses, and during the flight back to the States."

"You're coming with us?" one of the reporters asked.

"Yes," George replied. "You'll have the pleasure of my company as a passenger, and I'll have the pleasure of experiencing this new airline. Please let my associates know before you leave here this morning where you intend to go, and how you can be reached. We'll need a complete list of names, addresses, and phone numbers, including mobiles. In the meantime, I believe the hotel staff is eager to serve your breakfast. Enjoy your full English fry-ups."

George slipped into the vacant chair next to me.

"Full English fry-ups?" I said.

"Full English breakfast," he responded. "Also known here as a fry-up. Everything fried. Of course, most Brits avoid it these days in health consciousness and have cereal and yogurt for breakfast. But the hotels feel their guests want something authentic."

"And you, sir?" Seth asked.

"I love my fry-ups," George said with a chuckle. "Nothing like a proper, hearty breakfast to start the day."

While George's two assistants circulated among the tables, taking down names and contact information, the waitstaff served us heaping platters of eggs, bacon, sausage, tomatoes, fried bread, and mushrooms. Despite the grim event of the previous night, appetites were not diminished, and we attacked our fry-ups with gusto.

When the meal was over and people began leaving the room, George took me aside. "I have a copy of your schedule for the day and evening," he said. "Will you be following it?"

"I don't think so," I replied. "I'd like to have enough free time to spend with you."

"That certainly appeals, Jessica, but I'm afraid I'll be tied up virtually all day getting ready to accompany you back to Boston. I'm sure you've noticed the vultures waiting outside."

"The press."

"Yes. This is a big story here in the UK. Silverton's plans to introduce a new carrier to London generated lots of press. Now, with his demise, the stories will get even bigger, and more numerous. The pressure is on. I've been in touch with stateside law enforcement. It will truly be a hands-across-the-sea investigation."

"Then you do whatever it is you have to do, George. Actually, it might be more beneficial for me to spend time with the other passengers. I might learn something valuable."

"Best you stay clear of it," he said.

"Why? You allowed me to accompany you to the scene of the crime. I feel very much a part of this. Wayne Silverton came from Cabot Cove, and I was privileged to have been invited on the inaugural flight of his new airline. Someone with whom I crossed the Atlantic may have murdered him. I want to know who that was, and see him, or her, brought to justice."

"And I know better than to argue with you, Jessica. I will free myself for dinner."

"So will I."

Seth came up to us. "Looks like you two are scheming something big," he said.

"We always are," George said, with a wink. "Good to see you again, Doctor. I hope we have a chance to talk."

"Since you'll be on our flight home, I suspect we'll have lots of time for gab."

"I look forward to it," George said.

I walked George and his two associates outside where chaos reigned. The cramped, U-shaped area in front of the Savoy was chockablock with vehicles, some belonging to the police, others to the media. The elegantly attired doormen, and less decked out parking attendants, scrambled to maintain order and to keep traffic moving. George's Jaguar was parked directly in front. Limousine drivers in dark suits, white shirts, and ties stood to one side, holding signs indicating they were waiting for members of our large party. One explained to me that they'd had to park out on the Strand because of the logjam near the hotel.

George and I arranged to meet back at the hotel at six. He squeezed my arm and walked to the driver's side of his car. The doormen cleared a path for his car, and he made his way out to the Strand.

I returned inside to rejoin Seth, the Metzgers, and the Shevlins who were lingering over coffee. By this time, the lobby was swarming with press, and we decided the best way to avoid them was to keep to the timetable of tourist attractions that Wayne had set up for us. There were a number of choices presented to us on the schedule. We'd opted for a visit to The Charles Dickens Museum that morning. Lunch was free time. In the afternoon, we were to spend time at the Old Bailey, where we would be briefed by one of the court's judges on the differences between British and U.S. law. That there are any surprises many people, considering that our system of jurisprudence is based upon theirs. Mort had been disappointed to learn that Scotland Yard's famed Black Museum, in which thousands of exhibits from all sorts of crimes were housed and displayed for those with a special invitation, had been closed, its memorabilia warehoused until plans could be made for a reopening. I'd visited it a few years ago as George Sutherland's guest and found it to be the most chilling museum experience of my life. I especially recall one exhibit. It had to do with a teenage girl who was celebrating her birthday. A package arrived at her home with an unsigned card that read, "You'll be surprised how closely it brings things." Inside was a pair of expensive binoculars. When her father put the eyepieces up to his eyes and turned the focusing knob, needle-sharp, solid wooden stakes sprung from both eyepieces, penetrating his eyes and leaving him permanently blind. One of his daughter's former suitors, whom she'd jilted, was eventually convicted of the dastardly crime. In my opinion, no punishment could have been severe enough.

We were joined on the trip to the former home of Charles Dickens, the great Victorian novelist and playwright, by Churlson Vicks, Wayne's British partner in SilverAir, and a half dozen others, including three members of the travel press who'd been on the inaugural flight and had insisted they were entitled to stay with the party. I've made it a point to visit Dickens's house on Doughty Street on almost every trip I've made to London. Somehow, the experience of standing in the space where this literary giant created his best works seemed to be absorbed through my pores each time I was there, and sent me back to Cabot Cove brimming with creative energy. The house on Doughty Street was one of many homes Dickens had in London, but the only one to have survived. It was where he'd enjoyed one of his most productive periods. *Oliver Twist*, *Nicholas Nickleby*, and *Barnaby Rudge* were written there, and *Pickwick Papers* was completed at that address. I especially enjoyed reading letters written by Dickens to his agent, William Creech, and to his publishers, asking for money, a situation to which every writer, past and present, can relate. One such letter, framed and hung on the wall of Dickens's study, to Chapman and Hall, publisher of *Pickwick Papers*, reads: "When you have quite done counting the sovereigns received for Pickwick, I should be much obliged to you to send me up a few."

I smile every time I think of that letter.

We spent an hour in the Dickens Museum. Vicks and I ended up in the basement where many first editions of Dickens's works are housed. The rest of our party was on the upper floors; mementoes from Dickens's parallel theatrical career are displayed there.

"Got a minute?" Vicks whispered to me. "Lovely day out there. I thought some air would do us both good."

I didn't feel the need for fresh air at that moment, but agreed to accompany him outside. He was right; it was a spectacular, sunny day in London, the sky a clear cobalt blue.

"You obviously enjoy London," he said as we stood on the quiet street lined with quaint Georgian terraced houses.

"Very much. I just wish I had more time to spend here."

"More time to spend with your friend, the inspector?"

His question surprised me. "Yes, that too," I replied.

"You're obviously close to him."

"We're very good friends," I said, feeling a hint of resentment at this query into my private life.

"I understand you accompanied him to the crime scene last night."

"That's right."

"And?"

"And what?"

"What conclusions have you and your inspector friend come to about who killed Wayne Silverton?"

"We haven't—or at least I haven't reached any conclusions, that is. Besides, if Inspector Sutherland has some preliminary thoughts, I doubt he would share them with me. He's a highly respected professional."

"Nor would you share them with me if he had," Vicks said in an accusatory tone thay annoyed me.

"Correct," I said. "While we're on this unpleasant subject," I said, "perhaps you have some ideas to share with me."

"About Wayne's killer. Yes, I do have a few. And unlike you, I have no hesitation about imparting them, Mrs. Fletcher. You need not look any further than our esteemed partner, Mr. Salvatore Casale."

"Oh. Why is that?"

His laugh reminded me of some of my least favorite high school teachers. It was a dismissive laugh, as though to say, "You silly, naïve girl."

"Surely," he said, "you know of Sal's background."

"I know that he and Wayne were partners in some Las Vegas real estate ventures."

That laugh again.

"That's a genteel way of putting it," he said. "Sal's connections with your American gangsters are well-known."

"Not well-known to me," I said.

"I wouldn't expect a woman of your refinement to be aware of such things. Frankly, I don't relish having a partner with Sal's sordid background. I fought Wayne when he suggested bringing Casale and his tainted money into the deal to get SilverAir off the ground. I pointed out to Silverton that the banks might not be enthusiastic about lending huge sums of money to a company with a known mafioso on its board. But he was adamant. I've never known anyone quite as stubborn as Wayne Silverton. No, arrogant is more like it."

As Vicks delivered his condemnation of Mr. Casale and, by extension, Wayne, I thought of what George had said about Vicks and his own unsavory reputation. George had also brought up the allegation of Casale's mob connections back in the States. Here was a classic case of the pot calling the kettle black, although I had to admit to myself that everything I knew about Casale and Vicks was hearsay. I had no firsthand proof of either man's alleged wrongdoings, but I had no reason to doubt what George had said. I'd never known him to exaggerate even in the slightest.

I decided this sidewalk conversation wasn't going to produce anything of interest regarding Wayne's murder. But I was compelled to say before breaking it off, "Even if you are correct and Mr. Casale does have criminal connections—and that's by no means proved—it still isn't a reason to accuse him of murder."

"On the surface, you are quite right, Mrs. Fletcher. But if you add motive—I believe motive is always of primary interest in a murder case—if you mix into the equation that there was bad blood between Casale and Wayne, you have your important motive."

"And what motive was that?"

"Money, of course. Not only was Wayne stubborn and arrogant, he wasn't always aboveboard in his business dealings. He promised Casale and *his people* a great deal more for their investment than was actually delivered. And you know, I'm sure, that *his people* don't settle their grievances in a court of law. They take a more direct approach."

"And you, Mr. Vicks? Were you also dissatisfied with your investment?"

Before he could answer me, we were interrupted by the emergence of the rest of our party from the Dickens Museum.

"There you are, Jessica," Maureen Metzger said. "We've been looking all over the museum for you."

"Mr. Vicks and I decided to get some fresh air," I said. "It's such a lovely day."

"That it is," said Seth, taking a deep breath. "It's a truly fat day in London." Seth always referred to such splendid days as "fat."

"I'm going to be leaving you at this point," Vicks said. "It's been a pleasure. Enjoy the rest of your day—this 'fat' day as the good doctor calls it."

We watched him saunter up Doughty Street and disappear into a crowd of people at the corner.

"Nice fellow," Seth offered.

"Looks like a really successful businessman," Maureen said. "What were you talking about, Jessica? The murder?"

"Investments, actually," I said.

"Ooh. Did he give you any good tips?" she asked.

"Nothing I can use," I said, smiling at her.

I didn't want to fuel any speculation on the part of my friends, especially with members of the press within earshot. Even though the reporters traveling with us that morning covered travel and business, they were never far away, and I knew their instinct was to listen for a story. I didn't want to provide them with one.

Our driver dropped off various people at selected locations, saving the Cabot Cove gang for last. Knowing we would be free for lunch, I'd called an old and dear friend, Sally Bulloch, the general manager of the Athenaeum Hotel and Apartments on Piccadilly. The hotel's highly rated and popular restaurant, Bullochs, was named after Sally, a dynamic hostess who seems always to be everywhere within the hotel greeting guests. Many of these guests are familiar show business names, some of whom stay for months in the row of elegant apartments adjacent to the hotel. Sally assured me that we'd have a prime table in the restaurant, and she didn't disappoint. She was in the lobby when we arrived, bubbling over with enthusiasm, and led us across the handsome stone floor to our table at the rear of the attractively appointed room, its skylights allowing the striking red, blue, and green space to be bathed in sunshine.

Once we were seated, and I'd made all the necessary introductions, Sally asked me to join her back in the lobby.

"So, Jessica, who killed him?" she asked bluntly.

I had to laugh. "I love the way you ease into things, Sally," I said. "Who killed Wayne Silverton? I have no idea."

"It's all anyone is talking about today. Here's the founder of a spanking new airline killed in cold blood on the first flight. Have you been in touch with your chum, the handsome, dashing Yard inspector?"

I had to laugh again. "Nothing ever escapes that steel-trap mind of yours, does it? Yes, I have been in touch with George Sutherland and—"

"The papers say you accompanied him to the airport where the body was found."

I felt a blush rise to my cheeks. "Gorry, leave it to the press to make something of nothing."

"Gorry, huh? And you say we Brits talk funny."

"It's a Maine expression."

"You people from Maine talk funny." She cocked her head at me. "That was quite an unflattering snap of you I saw on the telly this morning, dearie. If the photographer had gotten any closer, he'd have been in your mouth."

"I haven't seen it," I said, "and based upon your judgment, I'd just as soon not. I'd better get back to the table. But before I do, my good friend, what do *you* hear that might shed some light on the murder?"

"Aha," she said. "You're up to your old tricks, solving murders when all you should be doing is writing novels about them." She became slightly conspiratorial. "Folks say that anything Churlson Vicks is involved with has to be questioned." She lowered her voice even more. "Is it true that the Mafia owns part of the airline?"

"I wouldn't know about that," I said, adding, "I spent the morning with Mr. Vicks."

"And?"

"Nothing to report. You're a doll for setting up lunch for us. See you later."

"The chef has your favorite rack of lamb ready. *Gorry*, it's good to know that Jessica Fletcher is on the case."

My laughter continued into the dining room and to the table where Jim Shevlin had ordered two bottles of Australian wine, and where an assortment of complimentary hors d'oeuvres had been delivered.

Lunch began as a lighthearted affair, considering that Wayne Silverton's murder had taken place less than twenty-four hours earlier. I suppose it represented a deliberate attempt on everyone's part not to dwell on such unpleasant subjects, especially over a meal. But the gravity of the killing soon outweighed our collective stab at gaiety.

"So, Jess, come on now, fill us in on what's going on with Wayne's murder," Maureen said.

"I really don't know much," I said.

Their expressions said they weren't buying it.

"No, I mean that," I said. "Obviously, everyone who was on the flight is a suspect. I don't think George is considering the possibility that it might have been someone who just happened upon Wayne while he sat in the plane. It had to be someone who knew him, and that includes all of us."

"I didn't do it," Jim Shevlin quipped, his hands to his heart.

"Oh, stop it, Jim," his wife, Susan, said. "It's nothing to make light of."

"I'm not making light of anything, but if we're all suspects, we have an obligation to declare our innocence. Isn't that right, Sheriff?"

"There's no need for anyone at this table to declare anything," Mort said. "We know none of us killed Silverton. But I have some thoughts about it that I bet Inspector Sutherland will want to hear."

We waited for him to elaborate. When he didn't,

Seth said, "Seems if you're goin' to make a statement like that, Mort, the least you can do is tell us what in the devil you meant."

Mort sat back, a satisfied expression on his broad face. "I'd best leave it for the inspector," he said. "You know, talk shop with somebody who'll understand what I'm saying."

I had to smile. I knew that Mort was somewhat envious of George Sutherland's position in Scotland Yard. George investigated major cases, not only in the United Kingdom but in cities around the world. When in his company, Mort sometimes felt the need to puff himself up. It was silly of him to feel that way. He was a fine sheriff with a solid history in law enforcement, including a stint in New York City, one of the toughest places on earth to effectively police. But I suppose there was a glamour associated with Scotland Yard, and George certainly cut a dramatic figure. I could have pressed Mort for what he was thinking, but decided against it. If he felt he should disclose his thoughts on the murder only to George— lawman to lawman—then so be it. But I have to admit I was curious, and knowing Mort as I do, I was confident that he'd eventually reveal his thinking to me, too.

It didn't take too long for that to occur. After lunch, we went to the lobby to say good-bye to Sally Bulloch. As we waited for her to come from her office, Mort confided in me.

"The way I figure it, Mrs. F.," he said, his voice low so the others couldn't hear, "is that Wayne was killed by a woman."

"And why do you say that, Mort?"

"Just makes sense, that's all," he replied. "Think about it. Here's this handsome rich guy who owns an airline. Must have had plenty of women in his life before—and maybe even during—his marriage to Christine. I don't know whether you caught the way he looked at the stewardesses on the flight."

"The flight attendants?"

"Right, flight attendants. Got to be politically correct. Well, he had the roving eye of a guy who's used to beautiful women falling all over him. Make sense?"

"Yes, it does, although a knife is not statistically the weapon of choice for a woman."

"Plenty of wives have used a knife to get rid of a philandering or abusive husband."

"You're right," I said. "No one should be ruled out based upon statistics. Do you have someone specific in mind?"

"Nope. But I'll pass along my theory to George."

"And I'm sure he'll appreciate every bit of input he can get, especially from a fellow lawman."

"That's what I figured, too."

After thanking Sally for her hospitality, we moved to the street where a tall, charming doorman in a fancy uniform opened the door to the limo that waited for us. We got in, and the driver headed for the Old Bailey, a more familiar name for London's Central Criminal Court. While my thoughts were on the meeting we'd have with one of the judges there and what we'd learn from him, I couldn't keep my mind focused exclusively on that. What Mort had said had merit.

The problem was that the one woman who took center stage in that scenario was Wayne Silverton's wife, Christine.

Chapter Eight

In the United States, lawyers routinely spend hours, sometimes days, prepping witnesses before they take the stand to testify. Under the British legal system, any barrister or solicitor caught doing that would be harshly reprimanded by the court. The British approach makes more sense to me. Prepping witnesses smacks of manipulation of the truth. Barristers are usually attorneys who plead cases in court. Solicitors generally perform out-of-court legal work. But recent changes in British law allow solicitors to do trial work, too, in most courts.

Another difference between our legal systems that I find fascinating has to do with the role of the judge in British criminal trials. Here, I much prefer the American way. In British criminal cases, the judge sums up for the jury the evidence that both sides have presented during the trial. This gives a British judge much too much power, in my estimation, to sway a jury to his evaluation of guilt or innocence.

These and other differences were explained to us by a kindly, elderly judge who, I was flattered to learn, had read many of my books.

We spent an hour at Old Bailey. Our limo was waiting on Newgate Street when we emerged. We quickly got into our seats, eager to return to the Savoy and do two things: get ready for whatever dinner plans had been made and see whether there were any new developments in Wayne Silverton's murder. I hadn't mentioned my intention to have dinner with George and was reluctant to do so. But the issue was forced when Seth asked, "What are we doing tonight for dinner?"

"I have tentative plans to meet George Sutherland."

"How exciting," Maureen said. "We can get the latest from the horse's mouth. Well, from the inspector's mouth."

"Be a good chance for me to discuss the case with him," Mort chimed in.

"Actually, I— Oh, wait a minute."

We stopped at a traffic light, and I saw out my window a shop with a sign announcing that it featured London's largest selection of knives.

"Could we pull over in front of that shop for a few minutes?" I asked the driver.

"Yes, ma'am."

"Where are you going?" Jim Shevlin asked.

"Into that store that carries knives," I said, opening my door and getting out. Mort and Seth followed, and we entered the shop, the tinkle of a bell alerting the proprietor to our arrival. The owner, a wizened little old man with tufts of white hair shooting straight up from his head, came from a back room. He wore a heavy, dark gray cardigan I was sure had kept him warm during the London bombings of World War II.

"May I help you?" he asked.

"Perhaps," I said, and mentioned that we were from the States.

His face lit up. "Always enjoy showing my wares to Yanks," he said. "I assume you're interested in knives for the kitchen. I have the largest and most diverse stock in the UK."

"Actually," I said, "I'm interested in a knife a woman can carry in her purse, you know, with a blade that folds into its handle."

He looked at me suspiciously but didn't say anything as he led us to a display cabinet with a glass top through which dozens of knives of that description were carefully laid out on green velvet.

"Yes," I said, "that's the sort of knife I'm looking for."

"Jessica, do you mind telling us why you want to buy a knife?" Seth said sternly.

"I will as soon as I find what I'm looking for," I said, continuing to peruse the selection beneath the glass. "How about that one?" I said to the shopkeeper. "I'd like to see that one."

The shop owner looked and sounded disappointed. "We have so many knives that are better than that one, madam. That knife is—well, how shall I say it? That knife is inexpensive and very common."

"May I see it?" I repeated.

He reluctantly opened the back of the case with a key and handed me my choice. The blade was open.

"Careful, Jessica," Seth said. "I don't fancy having to sew up your hand."

"I'll be careful, Seth," I said, turning the knife over to get a good look at both sides.

"Yes," I said to the shopkeeper, "this is the one I want. You say it's a common knife. I assume you mean that many sorts of people use it."

"Mostly people who don't know much about knives," he said, going to another counter where he prepared to wrap my purchase. "I sell a lot of these. Plenty of bobbies carry them along with their nightsticks, and I've had a fair number of military folks buy them. Airline pilots seem partial to this brand, too. I supply the pilots from British Air and Mr. Branson's Virgin Atlantic." He shook his head. "I try to get them to upgrade to a better knife, but they're stuck in their ways, I suppose."

" 'Stuck?' " Seth said, smiling.

"Poor choice of words," the shopkeeper said, returning the smile. "Or a good one."

I paid for the knife and we left the shop, my neatly

wrapped purchase under my arm. Once I was back in the limousine, the questions came about the knife and why I'd bought it.

"Promise that what I say will remain in this limo?" I said.

Nods of affirmation were given all around.

"I got a close look at the knife that was used to kill Wayne," I said. "Not the whole knife, just the handle. It had an interesting pattern, like the one I just purchased. At least it appears that way to me. It's the right size, too, based upon the visual calculation I made at the scene."

As we snaked through mounting London traffic, I unwrapped the knife and showed it to everyone. "Who would like it?" I asked.

I received puzzled looks.

"I don't need the knife," I said. "What's important is what we learned from that very nice shop owner."

"The old fellow said he sells lots of knives like this to airline pilots," Mort said, an expression of recognition crossing his face.

I nodded. "It may not mean anything," I said, "but every little bit helps. I'm sure we can learn more about it from Captain Caine."

"He wasn't at breakfast this morning," Seth said.

"No, he wasn't, nor was the flight attendant, Ms. Molnari. We'll probably see them back at the hotel."

"If you really don't want the knife," Mort said, "I'll be happy to take it from you. I like having them handy in the car and the office, you know, to cut a rope or open a carton."

"Then," I said, handing it to Mort as we pulled up in front of the Savoy, "it's yours. Just don't put it in your carry-on luggage."

"I'll make sure of that," his wife said.

We stood together in the hotel lobby, waiting for the elevator. Seth said casually, as though addressing no one, "I wonder who inherits Wayne's stake in SilverAir."

I'd been wondering the same thing. My assumption was that Christine would be Wayne's beneficiary, but that wasn't necessarily true. If it was, it added an additional motive for her to want Wayne dead, both to avenge his philandering ways and to become a rich widow. But everything was supposition at this juncture. There were many questions still to ask, and many answers to be gathered.

George had left a message for me on my suite's voice mail.

"Hello there, Jessica. I trust you've had a pleasant day at the Dickens Museum and the courts. I'm glad you took the opportunity not to think about such grisly things as murder, and were able to simply enjoy the city with your Cabot Cove chums. I've made a reservation for us at seven thirty. The restaurant is a particular favorite of mine; I'm sure you'll find it satisfactory." There was a long, thoughtful pause, as though he was summoning up the courage to continue. Finally, he said, "As much as I look forward to us spending a quiet dinner alone, I realize that you have obligations to those who've traveled with you from home. So, what I'm saying is that if you feel the need to include them in our dinner plans, it will be fine with me."

What a dear. Among many admirable traits, his sensitivity ranked high. I was sure he preferred that we dine alone—so did I—but he was always so quick to take into consideration the needs of others. He left numbers where he could be reached, including his cell number, which I already had. I dialed it.

"George, it's Jessica."

"Hello there," he said. "Good day?"

"Very. Yours?"

"Hectic, and hopefully productive. You got my message."

"Yes. About dinner, I—"

"You wish to have your friends join us."

"I'm torn."

"Don't be. I'll call and change the reservation to—how many?"

"Make it for seven people, although I don't know if the Shevlins will join us. I heard them say something about getting together tonight with British friends."

"However it works out is fine," he said. "I'll swing by the hotel at seven."

"We have the limo for the evening," I said. "We can pick you up."

"Happy to go with you in your hired car, but I'll come to the Savoy. Make it seven fifteen."

"I'll be waiting. And thanks, George, for understanding."

I changed into a robe and turned on the telly, as the British call television. I kept the sound low, more for background talk than to become informed of the day's news. I sat on the couch and perused magazines, and booklets about the hotel and its services, before heading for the bathroom and a leisurely shower. I'd just gotten up and was halfway across the room when Wayne Silverton's face filled the screen. I quickly raised the volume and resumed my seat.

The announcer delivered a brief recap of Wayne's murder, a bit of background about SilverAir, and quoted an unnamed police source who said that a full-scale investigation was under way, but that no breaks in the case had been reported. Then, to my surprise, Christine's photo came to life. She stood at a podium with a uniformed officer and spoke directly to the camera.

"The brutal murder of my husband has shocked everyone who knew him. He was struck down at the pinnacle of his dreams to form a new airline offering better service to millions of passengers. I call upon everyone watching me at this moment to come forward to the authorities if you have any information that might help apprehend his murderer. There is a vicious killer on the loose at Stansted Airport, and the sooner he is brought to justice, the safer everyone will be. Thank you."

I turned down the sound again and pondered what she'd said. Obviously, she was dismissing the possibility that someone close to Wayne was the murderer, pointing instead to a stranger having committed the crime. While that was a possibility, it was a remote one, and I wondered whether it truly represented what she believed, or if it had been said to divert attention from those who'd been with us on the flight.

The shower was hot and pleasurable, but my mind was on anything and everything but soap and water. Going into the knife shop and buying one had been strictly a whim on my part. The vision of the knife protruding from Wayne's upper back had stayed with me since witnessing it, and I'd felt almost compelled to hold a similar one in my hand.

But more important, whose hand had held the actual murder weapon and used it to take Wayne's life?

The only way to rid myself of that grim vision on the 767's flight deck was to come up with an answer.

Chapter Nine

As it turned out, I was right about the Shevlins having made other dinner plans. They were replaced in our party by former airline captain Jed Richardson and his wife. George arrived at the Savoy right on time, and we all headed off to the restaurant he'd chosen, Langan's Brasserie in London's posh Mayfair section.

"I think you'll like it," George said during the drive. "Michael Caine is a part owner, which ensures a smattering of celebrities on most nights, and the food is quite good."

"Ooh, how exciting," said Maureen. "I love his movies."

"I can do without so-called celebrities," Seth commented. "Food is what matters in a restaurant."

"Right you are," George happily agreed, aware from previous encounters with Seth that the evening would likely be peppered with such remarks.

George had mentioned to me earlier that Langan's

was a dressy sort of place, and I'd passed along that information to the others. Everyone had gussied up for the evening, as though setting out for a festive evening.

A festive evening.

I've always been impressed with how adaptable we human beings are at simultaneously handling pain and pleasure. The rituals we observe following the death of someone near and dear were, I'm certain, designed to allow this to happen. Whether a Catholic or Protestant wake, a Jewish shivah, or another gathering following a death, grieving is simultaneously balanced by joyous remembrances of the deceased; the resulting laughter mitigates the pain and turns such events into a celebration of life. Without such a release, unrequited grief might be too much to bear.

George concluded his minilecture about the restaurant by saying, "I have to admit that I have a particular fondness for Langan's. It serves the best steak tartare in London."

"Steak tartare," Mort said. "That's a favorite of mine, too—as long as it's well-done." He laughed at his little joke, and we laughed along with him.

Wayne Silverton's murder wasn't mentioned by anyone during the limousine ride. But once we were seated at a large table on the restaurant's cozy second floor, and drinks had been served along with appetizers—George was the only one to order the raw, ground steak, much to Seth's obvious facial expressions of displeasure—I asked Jed, "When you flew for the airline, did you and other cockpit crew members routinely carry a knife in your bags?"

Jed, who looked every bit the pilot, his face tanned and filled with lines from having looked into the sun for thousands of hours at high altitudes, nodded. "I don't know anyone who didn't," he said. "Of course, now lots of commercial pilots carry a handgun, too. I don't agree with that policy, but antiterrorism rules since Nine Eleven have changed many things: pilots carrying weapons, reinforced cockpit doors, most of it worthwhile. But not guns. Commercial pilots are busy enough safely flying the plane without also having to become marksmen in confined quarters."

"Was there a special sort of knife pilots carried when you were flying commercially?"

He thought for a moment before replying. "Not any specific brand, although they tended to look the same, a four- or five-inch blade that retracts into a handle, usually black, but not always."

"Jessica bought a knife like that today," Mort said to George.

He looked at me with raised eyebrows.

"I wanted to see how easy it was to buy a knife like the one used to kill Wayne."

"I suppose you've got prints by now off the murder weapon," Mort said to George.

"Ah, no, not that I'm aware of."

Mort gave George an *I understand* look. "Can't discuss an ongoing case," he said. "Maybe we can have a private talk a little later, lawman to lawman."

"Yes, that would be fine, Sheriff."

Seth was the next person to bring up the murder. He waited until our salads had been served. "I suppose you did a careful analysis of blood spatter at the scene," he said to George.

"Our evidence technicians did," George said. "They're good at what they do."

Seth then spoke of various forensic conferences he'd attended. While he took pride in being a simple, small-town physician, he assiduously kept abreast of medical advances by attending seminars in a variety of areas, including forensic medicine. He spoke about the newest techniques available to forensic physicians and medical examiners throughout the time we spent eating our salads and ordering entrées. I could see that George was impressed with Seth's knowledge and depth of understanding, and I took quiet pride in my Cabot Cove friend's performance.

We followed George's lead and ordered what's best described as bourgeois British classics, bangers and mash (sausage links and mashed potatoes), and bubble and squeak (fried pureed potatoes and cabbage), which George claimed were always superbly prepared. The meal didn't disappoint. Everyone's appetite was sated, and it took some gentle, humorous persuasion by the waiter to get us to order homemade desserts—three portions with multiple forks.

"Well," Mort said after we'd finished coffee, "how about we go somewhere for a nightcap?"

To which Maureen immediately responded, "I think Jessica and George would probably appreciate an hour or two to themselves. Isn't that right, Jess?"

"I—"

"That's a splendid idea," said George. "You folks take the limo back to the hotel. Have your nightcap in its American Bar. A lively place, to be sure."

I checked Seth's expression for his reaction to Maureen's suggestion. He smiled at me, winked, and said he wholeheartedly agreed.

We said our good nights in front of the restaurant, and George and I watched the limo pull away.

"I like your sheriff's wife more and more," he said, punctuating his words with a laugh.

"It was sweet of her to do that," I said.

"What's your pleasure?" he asked.

"Somewhere quiet where we can sip a drink, or coffee, and talk."

"My sentiments exactly, Jessica. Let me see. Ah ha, I have just the answer."

He hailed a passing taxi and we settled into the spacious rear compartment. Among many things I love about London are its taxicabs. The large, square, roomy vehicles are the most comfortable cabs in the world, and their drivers the most professional and knowledgeable. It takes years for a London taxi driver to obtain a license, years of learning every possible street, and the location of every hotel, restaurant, and tourist attraction, many of them impossibly obscure.

A few minutes later we pulled into a cul-de-sac in front of Dukes Hotel.

"I've stayed at Dukes before," I said. "I love it."

"Then you're aware of its unusual, small bar."

"I love that, too. So cozy. When I was here last, they offered tastes of rare cognacs and ports. The barman was charming. His name was—"

"Salvatore Calabrese."

"Yes. You know him."

"Quite well. He's no longer at Dukes. He now mans the Library Bar at the Lanesborough Hotel at Hyde Park Corner. London's most expensive hotel, I might add."

The small bar was empty when we walked in, except for a bartender shining glasses. He greeted us. We took a tiny table with two chairs in a far corner, looked at each other, smiled, and sighed. "Two cognacs," George told the barman when he came to the table, "but not your most expensive." George said to me, "Some of their cognacs go back more than a hundred years and cost a king's ransom for a taste. A month's salary."

"Any vintage is fine with me," I said. "What's important is that we're here together."

"Yes, that is what's important. So, Jessica, you've found yourself in the middle of a murder again."

"The way you say that, George, it sounds as though knowing me could be a health hazard."

He laughed. "If it is, I'll gladly put myself in jeopardy. I assume you're eager to learn what's new on my end regarding Mr. Silverton's murder."

"Only if you wish to tell me," I replied. "There are many other topics I'd be just as happy with."

"I'll get to those other topics after an update on the Silverton case. Your sheriff, Mort, asked about fingerprints. I didn't feel at liberty to discuss it with him, but I will with you. The prints found on the handle of the knife used to kill Mr. Silverton belong to the pilot who flew you here."

"Captain Caine?"

"Yes. His prints are on file in numerous places, given his military record and his career as a commercial airline pilot."

"I suppose I shouldn't be surprised," I said. "As you heard from Jed Richardson, all pilots carry a knife of one sort or another."

"Of the type you bought today?"

"Yes. As it turned out, I needn't have bothered. It never occurred to me to ask Jed whether pilots carry them. I assume you've spoken to Captain Caine."

"Briefly. On the phone this afternoon. I reached him at the hotel."

"And?"

"He's agreed to meet with me in the morning."

"Did you speak with one of the flight attendants, too, Ms. Molnari?"

"As a matter of fact, I did. She was in Captain Caine's suite when I called, and he offered to put her on the phone. It was almost as though he expected me to call and had her there purposely."

"Did you tell him about having found his prints on the murder weapon?"

"No. I thought I'd wait until seeing him in person. Let me see. Next? I had my team contact the major taxi companies to see whether any of their drivers took a fare from the Savoy to Stansted Airport last night during the hours between when your party arrived at the hotel and the estimated time of Silverton's death. There were two who said they had."

"Have the drivers been questioned?" I asked.

"Yes, by one of my staff. One said he drove a woman to the airport, the other a man."

"Did they know their names?"

"No."

"Could they ID them if they saw them again?"

"They both said they doubted it. According to the drivers, both passengers got in the back of their taxis, gave Stansted as their destination, and said nothing else during the ride."

"When they paid?"

George shook his head. "They might be claiming to have nothing to offer in order not to become involved. I should point out that these drivers work for fleets. There are hundreds of independent drivers who might have picked up other passengers at the Savoy at that same time. Finding them will be impossible."

Our cognacs were served in expensive crystal snifters, accompanied by glasses of water. We held up our glasses and touched rims. "To seeing you again, Jessica. If I haven't already said it, you look wonderful."

"Thank you, sir. I might say the same thing about you."

"To looking good," he said, smiling broadly. "To being the only two people on earth who never age."

We toasted to that, too.

"You said that Mr. Silverton's wife had told you something of interest," he said, sitting back in his chair and crossing one long leg over the other.

"That's right. As you know, I spent time alone with her after we'd broken the news about her husband's death. According to her, he was quite a philanderer."

George's eyebrows rose. "I assume she was not happy about that state of affairs," he said.

"Not at all. When I picked up her raincoat to put it in the closet, I noticed it was damp. And it looked like their four suitcases hadn't been opened."

"Meaning?"

"Meaning that she might not have been in the room very long. I'm obsessive-compulsive about unpacking the minute I get into a hotel room. I suppose I shouldn't impose my own particular habits on someone else, but I found it strange, that's all. She had hours to unpack—assuming she was in the room all that time. I don't think she was."

"Possibly one of the taxi fares to Stansted."

"Possibly."

"Well," he said, "now that we've covered what we know to date about the murder, let's get on to more pleasant things, namely us."

"I suppose I should apologize for what's gotten in the way of our having time together," I said.

"No apologies necessary, Jessica. You certainly aren't responsible for a murder having taken place, and as for your friends joining us tonight for dinner, I understand perfectly. But I must admit that spending so little time together is extremely frustrating. I realize that we live an ocean apart, and that we both lead busy professional lives. That's good, of course, and I wouldn't suggest that it be any other way. I've been content for all the years we've known each other to, as we say in Scotland, *Let the tow gang wi' the bucket.*"

I laughed. "I love your Scottish expressions, George, only I never know what they mean unless you tell me. It's a foreign language."

"Then I shall translate. What I said means simply that I have allowed things to run their course."

I sighed and extended my hands in a gesture of helplessness. "I don't think it's any mystery that I am very fond of you, George Sutherland."

"And I'm sure that you are aware that the feeling is entirely mutual."

I nodded.

"Your Frank was quite a man from what you've told me."

"Yes, he was. He was— Well, in many ways he was very much like you, George."

"I'm flattered, of course."

"As Frank got older, he often said that he'd become more liberal, not in a political sense, but in his acceptance of human frailties." I laughed. "That was one of many things I loved about him, his willingness to change his outlook on life."

"One of the few benefits of aging," George said, "is the wisdom that comes with it. I share your departed husband's philosophy. The more years I live, the more able I am to understand, even celebrate, man's foibles. Lord knows, we have enough of them."

"It must be especially difficult for someone like you, George, to practice that viewpoint."

"Why?"

"Because of what you do for a living. Coming into contact every day with man's baser instincts."

"It was more difficult earlier in my career, but you learn rather quickly to compartmentalize such things. Despite the evil in the world, there is so much more good to focus on. A prime example is having met you, Jessica. Little did I dream when we first met here in London all those years ago that our friendship would sustain itself the way it has." He lifted his snifter. "To my dear friend from across the pond."

I touched the rim of his glass with mine. "And to

you, Inspector George Sutherland. As the song lyric says, you light up my life."

"Which brings up something I've been meaning to say to you for some time now, Jessica."

"Yes?"

Suddenly, his cell phone rang. "Sutherland here. . . . I see. . . . Yes, of course . . . I'll be there in a matter of minutes."

He clicked his phone closed and replaced it in his jacket pocket.

"I take it we're leaving," I said.

"Immediately."

He motioned for the barman, who brought us our check. George laid cash on the table. "The cognac was excellent," he said as we left the bar, went outside, and climbed into the next available taxi.

"The Savoy Hotel," he told the driver.

"What's happened there?" I asked.

"The flight attendant Ms. Molnari has evidently attempted suicide."

Chapter Ten

An ambulance and two London patrol cars were at the front entrance to the Savoy when we pulled up.

"The hotel didn't know what it bargained for when it booked our party," I commented as we left the taxi and went inside where Mort Metzger stood talking with Cabot Cove's mayor, Jim Shevlin.

"We just heard about the flight attendant," I said.

"Where is she?" George asked.

"In her room," Mort said. "No, strike that. It's the pilot's room."

"Captain Caine," I said.

"Right," said Mort. "Seth is up there with her. There's a British doc, too."

"I'd best join them," George said.

He looked at me and knew what I was thinking. A nod from him said it was all right to accompany him.

After getting Captain Caine's room number, George and I rode up in the elevator together. I asked why he had been called to the scene of an apparent suicide attempt by a hotel guest.

"I've made it known at my office that anything untoward having to do with the SilverAir passengers should be reported to me immediately. Whether this young lady's act has anything to do with Mr. Silverton's murder is purely conjecture, of course, but it can't be dismissed out of hand."

Two uniformed officers standing outside Caine's door snapped to attention upon seeing George, who led me into the room where the flight attendant was on a couch in the sitting room portion of a small suite, a blanket covering her up to her neck. Seth Hazlitt, and another man I assumed was the British physician Mort had mentioned, hovered over her.

"How is she?" George asked.

The British doctor turned and frowned at this question from someone he didn't know.

"He's from Scotland Yard," Seth said.

George spared Seth an explanation by introducing himself and me.

"She'll be fine," the British doctor said, returning his attention to Molnari.

Seth took George and me aside and whispered, "An overdose, although not much of one. Made her sick but wasn't enough to kill her. The bottle's over there on that table."

"Seeking attention?" George asked.

"Possibly," Seth replied, "but that doesn't mean taking it less seriously."

"Who reported it?" George asked.

"The fellow in the bedroom," Seth said, "the airline pilot. This is his room."

I moved away from them to gain a view of the bedroom where Captain Bill Caine sat in a flowered wing chair by the window, his attention directed outside. I returned to Seth and George.

"Did he say what prompted her to come here to his room and attempt to take her life?" I asked.

"He hasn't said much since the doc over there and I arrived," Seth said. "Those two officers out in the hallway were here before that."

"She needn't be taken to hospital?" George asked.

"Might not be a bad idea to have her spend a night there," Seth offered, "and have a psychiatrist look in on her. Even if she was only calling out for attention, there's got to be something pretty heavy weighing on her."

"I think I'll have a word with Captain Caine," George said. "Jessica?"

I'd been looking around the room, my focus not on their conversation. "What?" I said. "Oh, yes, I'll come with you."

We entered the bedroom and George quietly closed the door behind us. Caine never looked up to acknowledge our presence. He continued to sit stoically, his eyes trained on something through the window—or perhaps on nothing.

"Excuse us," George said. "I'm Inspector George Sutherland, and you know Mrs. Fletcher, I believe.

We didn't have the pleasure of meeting this morning at breakfast, although we did speak by phone earlier today."

"Researching a plot for your next book?" Caine asked me.

George saved me from having to answer. "We'd arranged to meet tomorrow," he told Caine, "but since we're here, I wonder if I might have a word with you now."

Caine, who wore a silky, dark blue warm-up suit with white stripes down the legs, and sneakers, shrugged. "Hell of a time for a talk, isn't it?" he said. "Gina's in there hanging on to life, and you want to talk."

"According to the doctors with her," George said, "she'll be fine. However, if you prefer to wait until tomorrow to discuss Mr. Silverton's murder, I'm willing to do that. But I do have a few immediate questions about this episode tonight. I understand it was you who called to report the young lady's attempt to take her life."

"That's right. It's a good thing I did or she might not have made it."

"I don't doubt that," George said, not reiterating that whatever pills she'd taken would not have killed her. "This is your room, I believe."

"That's right."

"What prompted her to come to your room intending to commit suicide?"

Caine managed a smile. He needed a shave, and his hair wasn't as neatly combed as when he'd been in uniform and in command of our aircraft across the Atlantic.

"We're crew," Caine said. "Airline crews become close, like family. We're always in and out of each other's rooms."

That was contrary to what Christine Silverton had told me not long ago. She'd said that in her early days as an airline stewardess—those days that were the basis for the mildly racy book, *Coffee, Tea or Me?*—there was a great deal of fraternizing between members of a flight crew. Christine had also said that the myriad changes in the airline industry had developed a wall between cockpit and cabin crews. Captains and first officers tended to avoid spending layover time with flight attendants, unless—unless there was a romantic interest between them, a relatively rare occurrence these days, according to her.

"How long had she been here with you before she took the pills?" I asked.

Caine fixed me in a stony stare and said, "I knew you were a novelist and private pilot, Mrs. Fletcher, but I didn't know you were a cop, too."

"Oh, I'm not," I said, "but—"

"It's a perfectly reasonable question," George told Caine.

The pilot exhaled noisily, stood, and paced in front of the closed door. "Look," he said, "I had no idea when Gina came here that she intended to pull some dumb trick like this. I took a shower, and when I came out she was there on the couch, a mess."

"She seemed fine when she arrived?" George asked.

"Perfectly fine."

"What happened to change things?" I asked, injecting as much concern as possible into my voice to take the edge off sounding like, well, a cop.

For a moment, it appeared that he wouldn't answer me. But he sat in his chair again, shook his head, and gave forth a small smile. "We had an argument," he said.

"About?" George asked with elevated eyebrows.

"It's personal," Caine said.

"Very well," George said. "Tell me about the pills, Captain. You had them here, in your room?"

"No. She must have brought them with her."

I believe George was thinking what I was thinking, that it would be highly unusual for a person contemplating suicide to bring her own pills to someone else's room. People intent on taking their life generally prefer to do it alone.

George put that thought into words.

Another shrug from Caine. "How the hell am I supposed to answer that?" he growled. "It's nuts enough trying to kill yourself. Why did she bring the pills here? I haven't the slightest idea."

"Has she been depressed lately?" I asked after a lull in the conversation.

"She's a woman," Caine replied. "Always up and down, happy one minute, unhappy the next. I don't think she was any more depressed than the average person, whatever that is."

I held my tongue.

"Well," George said, "I appreciate your time, Captain. I would like to have our talk tomorrow concerning the murder."

"Sure. You're wasting your time. I don't know anything about Silverton being killed, but ask all the questions you want."

"May I use your bathroom?" I asked.

"Help yourself."

When I came out of the bathroom, George was ready to leave. He opened the door and we started into the sitting room. But he stopped, turned, and said, "I understand most commercial airline pilots carry a knife among their possessions."

Caine cocked his head and frowned. "A knife?"

"Yes. I'm sure it comes in handy now and then. I carry one myself." George reached into his jacket pocket and withdrew a small knife, its handle no longer than a few inches. He pulled the blade from the handle, the same length. He laughed and secured the blade in the handle again. "I believe the last time I used this was to sharpen the point on a pencil."

Caine smiled. "Ah, yes, I see where this is going, Inspector. Do I carry a knife? Of course I do. But for your information, it wasn't the one used to kill Silverton."

"I didn't suggest that it was," George said.

I'd stepped back into the bedroom.

"You ever have anyone knifed to death in your novels, Mrs. Fletcher, or do you prefer less violent murders?" Caine asked.

"Some of my characters have used knives," I said. "It depends upon the circumstances, doesn't it?"

The pilot went to the closet, opened the door, and pulled out a square black leather case on wheels. He pulled it to the chair, sat, sprung two metal latches on its top, and reached down inside. "Here's my knife," he said while still rummaging through the case, "and not a drop of blood on it."

George and I waited for him to produce the weapon. His digging through the case's contents became more hurried and intense. Finally, he withdrew his hand, looked at us, and said, "It's not here."

"Perhaps you forgot to pack it this trip," George suggested.

"It's not here," Caine repeated. "And I did pack it. I know I did. It's always in this case, has been for years. I can't imagine what—"

"I'm sure there's a good reason for it being missing," George said. "We won't take any more of your time, Captain. Until tomorrow."

George shut the door behind us. Gina Molnari was now sitting up on the couch, the blanket covering her lap. "No, I'll be fine," she said to Seth and the British doctor. "It was a mistake, that's all. I hadn't been sleeping well and thought a couple of pills would help me. I must have taken too many."

"Why here, in this room?" I whispered to George.

He said nothing.

"I still think it would be wise for you to check into a hospital overnight," Seth said. The British physician nodded his agreement.

"No," Gina said, standing. "I'll be fine. I just need to get some sleep."

"Can't force her," Seth said to me.

Seth and his British counterpart escorted her to her room, which was next door to Captain Caine's.

"We might as well leave," George said.

I agreed, and we started for the door. But I retraced my steps to the small table next to the couch on which the bottle of pills rested. I picked it up. It was a prescription for sleeping tablets. At least Gina hadn't taken them with her, I thought, and joined George in the hallway where he'd dismissed the uniformed officers.

"Sorry our pleasant time together was interrupted," he said as we entered an elevator.

"Life is unpredictable," I said.

"Which can be good and bad," he said.

We reached the lobby.

"Care to continue our quiet drink together?" he asked.

"I don't think so, George. I'm suddenly exhausted, as though a plug has been opened on my energy tank. Why did you raise the question of the knife? I thought you'd decided to wait until tomorrow to mention the prints found on it.''

"Oh, I thought I'd give him something to think about tonight.''

"I'm sure he'll give it plenty of thought. He said he'd taken a shower when Ms. Molnari took the pills. I don't think he did. Every towel in his bathroom is bone dry.''

George smiled. "You should come to work for the Yard,'' he said.

"Where do I apply?''

"I understand your fatigue, Jessica. I'll leave you to enjoy a good night's sleep.''

I looked past him to see Seth, the Metzgers, and the Shevlins come up a stairway and head in our direction. "Good night,'' I said fondly to George.

George started for the main entrance, and I took a couple steps toward my friends. But I stopped and called after George, who came back to me.

"I should have mentioned,'' I said, "that the sleeping pills Ms. Molnari took were a prescription.''

"Yes. I would think as much.''

"But the prescription wasn't written for her. They were for Christine Silverton, Wayne Silverton's wife.''

Chapter Eleven

Sleep?

As tired as I was, sleep was out of the question. I'd been embroiled in murders before. But as I got ready for bed and tried to fall asleep, my eyes remained wide-open, my mind in overdrive, my body rejecting my attempts to keep it in a prone position.

I finally gave up, slipped into my robe and slippers, and called room service: "A pot of tea, please, and a plate of cookies." Everyone has their individual ways of coping with stress and brain overload. Mine is a cup of tea and cookies. Yes, cookies of any sort, chocolate, vanilla, crunchy, or soft. It doesn't matter. Cookies soothe me. Fortunately for my waistline, the need for a cookie prescription doesn't happen that often.

Those who know me are aware that besides finding an occasional batch of cookies to be calming, I'm also obsessive-compulsive about the power of writing things down to help clear the mind. I'm an inveterate list maker. Seeing things in black-and-white on a sheet of paper brings clarity to my thinking. And so I sat at the ornate desk and wrote down everything I could remember from the moment I arrived at Logan Airport in Boston, up through this moment in my suite. The list of thoughts and observations was long, and I tried to create a pattern into which various items could be placed, one possibly having something to do with another. I ended with a long series of questions to be answered; answer those questions and I'd conceivably know who'd murdered Wayne Silverton.

I pulled out the schedule for the rest of our time in London. There were a few planned activities that had to be signed up for, some of which had interested me earlier. But I decided not to tie myself down.

The flight back to Boston would leave Stansted at ten the next night. That gave me a full day and part of the evening to seek answers to those questions. In a sense, time would work in my favor. Unlike other murder investigations with which I'd become involved, albeit reluctantly, this one would find all the possible suspects still gathered together, in this instance in the confines of a modern jet airliner. Unless, of course, someone decided to bolt and not take the return flight. I considered that unlikely. Anyone who opted out of getting on the plane would immediately focus a spotlight on himself as the most likely of suspects. No, I was confident that everyone who'd flown with us to London would be on SilverAir's 767 back to Boston.

Of course, the mood on the return flight was bound to be less festive than the atmosphere on the flight to London. George would be aboard asking questions and, unlike other venues in which suspects are grilled, while streaking through the dark sky at thirty-five thousand feet above the cold Atlantic, there would be nowhere to go to avoid having to answer.

At times like this I found myself wishing sleep wasn't necessary. I felt the pressure of having less than twenty-four hours left in London and was eager to make optimum use of the time. But I also knew that if I didn't get some sleep, the next day would be painful. I climbed into bed and tried to will myself to sleep. That didn't work, of course, so I practiced some self-hypnosis techniques that Seth had taught me—eyes rolled up into their sockets, relaxing every part of my body, beginning with my toes and gradually working up to my head. It worked. I was asleep.

When I awoke, I was certain I'd slept for no more than an hour, but the clock said differently. I'd had five hours of solid rest, and I got out of bed feeling rejuvenated and ready to tackle the day. There was no formal breakfast gathering scheduled, which pleased me. I showered, dressed casually and comfortably, and headed downstairs for some breakfast. Seth, the Metzgers, and the Shevlins were already in the dining room.

"You look surprisingly chipper," Seth said.

"I used your hypnosis tips, Seth. They worked."

"Of course they did. I wouldn't have bothered teaching them to you if they didn't."

"So, what's new with the murder?" Maureen asked.

"Or the suicide," Susan Shevlin added.

"Not much on either front," I said. "I assume Seth has filled you in on what happened with Ms. Molnari."

"Not much," Maureen said, sounding unhappy about it.

"Doctor-patient privilege," Seth said.

"Oh, come on, Doc," Mort said, "you're with friends. Besides, I'm a law enforcement officer."

"I told you everything of importance," Seth said as a waiter arrived and took our orders.

Seth had brought that morning's edition of the paper with him to breakfast, and he unfolded it. "Well, now, look at this," he said, pointing to an article below the fold on the front page.

The headline read: THE SOPRANOS INVADE LONDON.

"What's it about?" Jim Shevlin asked.

Seth read the piece, his brow furrowed, an occasional grunt coming from him. Finished reading, he passed the paper to me.

"The plot thickens," I said after reading it and handed the paper to Maureen.

The article reported how local police, in concert with Scotland Yard, had intercepted and detained two men at Heathrow Airport. According to the piece, an international all-points bulletin had been issued for these men, reputedly members of an organized crime family back in the United States. They were accused of being hit men for the mob, with a long string of alleged murders of other mob figures as part of their dossier. While this made for interesting reading, it was the final paragraph that really captured my attention:

In a related matter, the two individuals who were taken into custody are also reputed to be involved with Salvatore Casale, a partner in the new airline SilverAir, which only recently made its inaugural flight to London. As reported in this paper, Mr. Casale's partner and founder of the start-up airline, Wayne Silverton, was found brutally murdered in the cockpit of his 767 aircraft at Stansted Airport. Mr. Casale's business base of operations is reported to be in Las Vegas, Nevada, where he is involved in real estate transactions. The murder victim, Mr. Silverton, is reported to have been involved with Mr. Casale in many of these real estate deals. Scotland Yard, which is investigating the Silverton slaying, declined to comment on this ongoing case.

"I knew it the minute I met him," Maureen said.

"Knew what?" I asked.

"That he was a mobster."

"Why?" her husband asked. "Because he's Italian?"

"Of course not," she said, defensively. "I didn't know then that he was Italian. But you only have to look at him. There was something in his eyes, something ruthless."

"If I could identify mobsters simply by the expression in their eyes," Mort said, "I could get a great job with the FBI."

"But then we'd miss you in Cabot Cove, Sheriff," I said, winking at Maureen. But silently, I agreed with her observation about Mr. Casale's eyes. They were hard, dark eyes, lacking any mitigating compassion.

"Well," I said, "what's on everyone's agenda today?"

"We thought we'd tag along with you, Mrs. F.," Mort said. "You know London better than we do. You've been here so many times."

It was not what I wanted to hear. Had I been totally honest with my friends, I would have said that I needed to be on my own for the day. Instead, I said, "How about this? I have some errands to run this morning that would just bore you, so why don't we head off in different directions and meet up for lunch?"

"What sort of errands?" Mort asked.

I was formulating an answer when Christine Silverton, accompanied by Sal Casale, entered the dining room. I waved to her to join us. She and Casale said something to each other before he walked away, and she came to our table.

"Please join us," I said.

She took the one empty chair.

"How are you this morning?" Seth asked, his tone that of a physician visiting a hospitalized patient.

"As well as can be expected," she said, "considering what's happened."

She was smartly dressed in a tailored taupe pantsuit, accented by a scarf in subtle hints of red and purple. She wore the barest hint of makeup, and her only jewelry was her wide, gold wedding band.

"If there's anything we can do, all you have to do is ask," Maureen said.

"Maybe you can talk sense to the police," was Christine's reply.

"What do you mean?" Mort asked.

"They won't release Wayne's body," she said, her anger palpable. "I wanted to have the body return to the States with us tonight, but Scotland Yard says it has to remain here in the UK for further autopsy tests."

That didn't surprise me at all, nor, I was sure, did Seth find it unusual. A murder had been committed. While family needs are always considered in such cases, the requirements of law enforcement trump any personal preferences. I didn't express what I was thinking, however. She didn't need a contrary opinion at this juncture.

Christine ordered juice, coffee, and a dry English muffin. Her eyes went to the open newspaper and the story about the detaining of the two men at the airport, and the possible link to Casale.

"Can you believe that?" she said, waving at the paper.

"You've seen the article on Mr. Casale?" Maureen asked, closing the tabloid so the front page was face-down on the table.

"I read it this morning in my room. Piece of trash. All lies. These media vultures are despicable."

"They've got a job to do," Seth offered.

Christine's nostrils flared. "A job? All they care about is making money off somebody else's misfortune and sullying every reputation they can."

"Has Mr. Casale seen it?" Mort asked.

"Of course. He's furious. He's considering bringing a libel suit. I hope he does. They shouldn't be allowed to get away with m—" She faltered. "To get away with publishing lies."

"Sounds like he's a good friend," Mort said.

Christine stiffened. "He has been a good friend," she said with emphasis, "—to Wayne. Wayne relied on his honesty and judgment and Sal never steered him wrong." Her eyes began to fill, but she dashed away the tears before any moisture touched her cheek.

Christine's defense of her husband's business partner was admirable. She was very emotional, understandably given the circumstances. I wondered whether Sal Casale was indeed the victim of an over-zealous press and if he really was the upstanding citizen Christine depicted. It would be interesting if he brought a libel suit. If he did, I thought, he'd have an easier time of it in England than back in the United States. Libel laws in Great Britain weigh heavily in favor of the plaintiff. The defendant, in this case a British newspaper, must prove it did *not* commit libel, as opposed to U.S. law where the plaintiff has the obligation to prove he or she *was* libeled.

The waiter arrived with Christine's breakfast. She took a sip of juice, then did the same with her coffee.

"Did you get some sleep last night?" I asked.

"I don't think I slept more than ten minutes at a time," she said.

"Is there anything I can do to help you today?"

"No, but thank you, Jessica." She dabbed at her lips with her napkin, and pushed back from the table, the muffin untouched.

"Not eating?" Seth asked.

"I don't have much of an appetite," she said. "Besides, I have a meeting to get to."

A meeting? I thought. *At a time like this?*

"We've got to work out the legal and financial tangles left by Wayne's death," she explained, standing. "And, of course, the police want to talk to me. You'd think I had something to do with the murder, the way they act. Sorry to run, and thanks for all your support. I don't know what I'd do without friends like you."

We said nothing as we watched her leave the dining room. Seth broke our silence.

"She should have eaten something," he said. "She needs nourishment."

"Maybe it's better that she keep busy with business matters," Mayor Shevlin offered. "Keep her mind off losing her husband."

While there was a certain validity to what Jim suggested, I had trouble squaring Christine's behavior with the tragic event that had taken place. Then again, I reminded myself, don't judge how other people react to tragedy.

"Wasn't it nice that she thinks of us as her friends?" Maureen said.

"What do you mean, Hon?" Mort asked.

"Well, we don't really know her all that well."

"Wayne and I go back a lot of years," Seth said, "but I can't say I knew the man or even liked him very much." He caught my eye. "Don't look at me like that, Jessica Fletcher."

"Like what?"

"I know what you're thinking."

I raised my eyebrows. "You do?"

"You're thinking I shouldn't speak ill of the dead."

"It's always a good policy," I said.

"Well, I told you I thought he was a slick one. Don't know why he even invited us, unless he wanted something."

Oh dear, I thought, *Seth's stuck his foot in it now.*

"I think he wanted to do something nice for his

hometown, for Cabot Cove," Jim said, frowning. "There certainly isn't anything I could have done for him as mayor—other than cheer him on. If I thought he wanted something from me, I would never have come."

Seth's eyes sought mine. I looked up at the ceiling, my lips pursed.

Susan put a hand on her husband's arm. "I'm sure Seth didn't mean anything by that, Jim," she said.

Seth coughed. "Certainly not!" he sputtered. "Sorry if you thought I was impugning your integrity, Mayor. Meant no such thing. It's the dead man's integrity I wonder about. That's all."

Good heavens. He's making it worse. If I'd been sitting next to him, I could have nudged him with my elbow or kicked his shoe. But we were on opposite sides of the table.

"You'll be seeing George today, I assume," Seth said, thankfully changing the topic of conversation.

"Oh, yes," I said. "I believe so."

I was hoping to accompany George when he interviewed Captain Caine. Christine had said the police wanted to talk with her. I wondered if George had already made an appointment to take her statement, and, if he had, when that would be. He was appropriately sensitive when first encountering her the night of the murder, but there would come a time— and rather quickly, I was sure—when he would want a full accounting of her movements leading up to the time Wayne was killed, and to gain what insights she had that might help point to the murderer. I decided that I would call his cell phone the minute I had time alone.

After a spirited discussion that lasted through breakfast, my friends decided to take in the changing of the guard at Buckingham Palace.

"Where are we meeting for lunch?" Mort asked me.

"Let's see," I said. I was tempted to return to the Athenaeum, but felt the others would probably want to experience something new. "I have it," I said. "We should have lunch at a genuine London pub before leaving, and I know just the one, the Grenadier."

"I like the sound of that, Mrs. F.," Mort said. "A grenadier is a soldier. Right?"

"Yes. A member of the British Grenadier Guards," I said. "The pub goes back to the early eighteen hundreds and is absolutely charming."

"How's the food?" Seth asked.

"Very good," I said. "And the place has a resident ghost."

"No ghosts for me," Maureen said with an exaggerated shiver.

"He's very well mannered," I said. "He was one of the Duke of Wellington's guardsmen who was flogged to death for cheating at cards."

"Served him right," Mort said, laughing.

"Where is it?" Jim asked.

"In a charming mews complete with cobblestones, right near Hyde Park Corner. You can't miss it.

There's a sentry box outside from when the duke used it as an officer's mess. How's one o'clock? Does that suit everyone?"

We agreed to meet there, and I watched them leave the hotel for their morning's adventures. I immediately called George's cell number.

"Good morning, Jessica," he said, the sound of his voice reassuring.

"Good morning to you, George."

"Where are you?"

"At the hotel. I was wondering whether we'd be catching up with each other this morning."

"Absolutely. I'm counting on you to play Dr. Watson to my Sherlock Holmes."

I smiled. "It would be my pleasure."

"Good. My appointment with Captain Caine is at eleven, right there at the Savoy. And Mrs. Silverton . . ."

I heard him riffling through the pages of his notebook.

"Let's see. Ah, yes. She's agreed to meet with me at three. Are you available at those times?"

"Even if I weren't, I'd change my plans to make it work."

"That warms my heart."

"George, there was an article in this morning's newspaper," I started.

"I think I know the one you mean."

"Those two men who were detained at Heathrow?"

"Yes. I read it."

"It's alleged that they're associated with Wayne Silverton's partner in the airline, Salvatore Casale."

"Interesting scenario, isn't it?" he said. "Makes one wonder whether they were here in the UK on an assignment."

An assignment to murder, I thought.

"You're exactly right," George said, reading my mind.

"I am?"

"You're thinking they could be involved in the murder. It's something we can discuss when we get a minute."

I was beginning to think I must have a transparent mind since both Seth and George were so adept at reading my thoughts.

"In the meantime," George was saying, "I just left one of the flight attendants who worked your plane."

"Ms. Molnari? Or Mrs. Scherer, the first officer's wife?"

"Wrong on both counts. Mr. Slater, the gentleman flight attendant."

"Was the interview fruitful?"

"In some ways, yes. He says he was the last crew member to leave the aircraft, although he does claim to have taken the crew limo into the city along with most of the others."

"'Most of the others,'" I repeated. "Who wasn't in that limo?"

"As you reported, the good captain wasn't among them. You saw him at the airport much later."

"That's right."

"It seems Ms. Molnari wasn't in that limo, either, at least according to Mr. Slater."

"Perhaps she was with Captain Caine."

"I'd say that's a logical possibility. I'd better ring off. Things to do before the eleven o'clock with Captain Caine."

"We'll meet here at the hotel a few minutes before then?"

"Exactly. Depending upon how it goes, we can grab a bite to eat following it."

"I'm afraid I've made lunch plans with my friends. I'd love you to join us, George. We're going to the Grenadier."

"Good choice. They make the best Beef Wellington in all of London. Afraid I can't tie up that much time. But you enjoy, Jessica. Until eleven."

I checked my watch. I had a little less than two and a half hours before meeting George. I stood in the Savoy's lobby, debating where to go first when Christine Silverton came storming up the stairs, anger written all over her face. She spotted me, seemed to go through an internal debate, and finally came over to me.

"What's wrong?" I said.

"God, I cannot believe these people."

"What people?"

"The low-life good-for-nothings Wayne got himself involved with to launch the airline. They are . . ." She shook her head as though that would shake out the words she was seeking. "They are crooks and scoundrels."

"I'm sorry you're so upset," I said, not knowing what else to say. "I take it the disposition of Wayne's participation in SilverAir is not going smoothly."

"Not if they have *their* way," she barked, her pique rising to another level. "It's bad enough that my husband has been brutally murdered by some madman. Now his so-called partners are already fighting over the spoils, vultures enjoying roadkill." Her voice was raised in anger and many in the lobby were turning to stare.

"How about a cup of tea together?" I suggested, taking her arm and ushering her toward the dining room. "It'll help you calm down."

She hunched her shoulders and blew a long stream of air through her lips. "I think I'd better get back to that meeting. No! They can't do anything without me. A cup of tea. Yes, that would be nice."

We found a small table with comfortable chairs in the upper dining room where the hotel serves afternoon tea. A waiter delivered a pot of Earl Grey, and a small plate of scones, which I was happy to see. Christine seemed to have simmered down considerably. She even managed a small smile after taking a sip. "Thank you, Jessica," she said. "I needed this."

"You're under such incredible strain," I said, "losing your husband, and having to deal with business issues so soon. Can't these discussions be put off, at least until you're back in the States and have had a chance to deal with your personal sorrow?"

She sighed and closed her eyes. When she opened them, she said, "You didn't know Wayne the way I did, Jessica. He was a driven man with little or no time for such trifles as personal sorrow or other human emotions. It was all business, and I know he'd want me to forge ahead as though nothing has happened. Once, when we were discussing death, he said, 'Dying is the price you pay for living. You're born, you die, and whoever is left had better get on with it.' " It was a rueful smile. "He'd be furious with me if I caved in just because he's no longer here."

"I've known other people like that," I said. "My husband, Frank, was a man who wanted those he loved to get on with their lives, and I've tried to do that since his death. But I also took some time to grieve. I'm glad I did."

"I know," she said. "It's just that—"

When she didn't continue, I said, "Men like Wayne go through life accomplishing many wonderful things. At the same time, they tend to make enemies along the way. Do any of Wayne's enemies come to mind as being capable of murdering him?"

This time her laugh was sardonic. "They'd fill a phone book," she said.

"That bad?"

"I'm afraid so. Of course, those who went into business with him were willing to overlook their per-

sonal feelings in the interest of making money. Casale and Vicks are two good examples. They've
accused Wayne of reneging on promises he allegedly
made to them, and they're not the only ones. That's
where I've been this morning, trying to sort things
out. Wayne's untimely death has created a rat's nest
of issues, including who ends up with his share of
the airline."

My raised eyebrows indicated my surprise. "I
would have assumed that the question of succession
would have been clearly spelled out in any
agreements between the parties," I said.

"It depends on which agreements you honor.
Wayne and I had a prenuptial agreement. There was
also his will. Both left whatever stake he had in his
various businesses to me. The will was redrawn just
before he started SilverAir, and specifically leaves his
share of the airline to me. But he also signed various
agreements with his partners giving them the rights
of succession. Which papers rule? I'm afraid this is
going to end up in a very long and drawn out
legal fight."

"What a shame," I said.

"That's an understatement."

I hesitated before saying, "Do you think one of his
partners killed him?"

"It wouldn't surprise me at this point."

"Which one?"

"Which one wanted to kill him? I have no idea.
Maybe all of them."

The waiter poured a second cup of tea, and I used the interruption to collect my thoughts. "As long as we're sitting here, Christine, would you mind if I asked you something? I have a couple of questions."

"I thought your handsome Scotland Yard inspector would be the one asking questions, Jessica. I'm seeing him at three."

"I know, but you could help me put to rest a few things that have been on my mind."

She made an overt act of checking her watch. "Go ahead, but make it fast."

"I don't know if you've been told about Ms. Molnari's suicide attempt."

She guffawed. "From what I heard, it was a pathetic attempt to get attention and sympathy."

"That may be," I said. "But aside from her motives, the sleeping pills she took were a prescription."

"And?"

"They were your sleeping pills, Christine. Your name was on the label on the bottle."

"Mine? That's absurd!"

"I saw it myself," I said. "I thought perhaps that's why you couldn't get much sleep with your pills missing."

She didn't respond, but took a sip of her tea.

"How do you suppose she came to have them?" I said.

"I haven't the slightest idea. What other question did you have?"

"I'm sorry to raise this topic, especially at this time,

but last night you mentioned that Wayne was not a faithful husband. Did his infidelities involve Ms. Molnari, or anyone else on the flight?"

"I think you've just stepped over the line, Jessica. Wayne's private life, and mine, shall remain just that—private."

"And I respect that," I said. "But indulge me one favor, Christine. Check your belongings to see whether any prescription pills you might have traveled with are still in your possession."

She smiled. "If it will make you happy."

"It will," I said, returning the smile.

"I have to go," she said. "Thanks for the tea and the break, and for helping me calm down a little. I think I'll get a breath of fresh air."

"I'll leave with you," I said, signing for our refreshments. "I need a walk and some fresh air, too."

We went outside together where the usual hectic activity was taking place, cars coming and going, people waiting for the valets to bring their vehicles, luggage being loaded on trolleys for delivery to guest rooms, the doormen chatting with hotel guests, giving directions, and greeting new arrivals. It was a lovely day in London, crisp and clear, the sky above a cobalt blue. I drew in a deep breath and held it for as long as I could.

Christine looked up at the sky regretfully. "I'd better get back inside to meet with the vipers again."

"I don't envy you that," I said.

"Take your walk, Jessica, and I—oh, my God."

A voice called out to her. We looked in the direction from which it had come and I saw a tall, lanky young man approaching. He wore a black leather jacket over a black T-shirt, jeans, and black sneakers. His dark hair was cut short, almost a buzz cut. He was swarthy, his facial features finely crafted.

"Oh, no," Christine whispered.

"Hello, hello, hello, Christine," he said when he reached us. "You look surprised to see me."

I looked at Christine for an answer to who he was.

"It would be polite, Christine, to introduce me to your friend."

"Why are you here, Jason?" Christine asked.

"Why, to see you, of course. I heard what happened to Dad." He grimaced. "What a terrible way to go." He turned to me. "Since my stepmother won't introduce us, I'll do the honors. I'm Jason Silverton. And you are?"

"Jessica Fletcher," I said, accepting his outstretched hand.

"The writer!" To Christine: "You're moving in better circles these days."

Christine's face was as hard as stone. "Why are you here?" she asked more strongly this time.

He flashed a wide smile, cocked his head, and answered, "Now that I own an airline, I thought I'd better show up. The first step toward success, as Woody Allen once said, is showing up. Well, Christine, dearest, here I am."

Chapter Twelve

We've all seen photographs of actors or actresses portraying a range of emotions—grief, anger, sadness, and joy. But no actor or actress could possibly exhibit *shock* as effectively as Christine Silverton did at that moment. Her mouth was slightly open, her eyes wide, her brow creased. She stared at Jason, seemingly wanting to say something but incapable of uttering the words.

"I know you're surprised to see me, Christine," Jason said, "but I did expect a warmer greeting after all these years."

"You?" she managed. "You own an airline?"

"That's probably the biggest surprise of all," he said.

Someone leaned on a car horn, causing Jason to wince.

"Let's go inside where it's quieter," he suggested.

"I—" Christine struggled to express her thoughts at the moment, but failed. She swirled away from us and entered the hotel, leaving me alone with this young man who claimed to be her stepson.

"Tsk. Tsk. No 'How are you?' No 'So sorry about your dad.' Not even a 'Would you like some tea, Jason?' Not exactly a warm welcome, is it?"

"I am very sorry about your father," I said. "It must have been a terrible shock for you."

"Just terrible," he said, but his tone was sarcastic. "A cup of coffee, Mrs. Fletcher?" He cocked his head. "Or maybe tea. We are, after all, in jolly old England. Frankly, I've never gotten into the tea habit since moving here. A cup of strong, black coffee is more to my liking. But I understand if—"

"Your sudden arrival has obviously upset your stepmother," I said, "and she's had her share of upsets lately."

"Of course," he said, "the grieving widow and all that sort of thing. She's good at playing roles. That's how she trapped my father."

"I think I would like a cup of tea," I said, "and you can have your coffee."

"Wonderful! I didn't come here expecting to enjoy the company of a world famous writer. Murder mysteries, aren't they? I'm not much into murder mysteries—science fiction is more my thing—but maybe you can convert me."

A doorman held open a door for me. I was halfway through when I turned and said to the smug young man who hadn't moved, "Coming?"

He followed me inside, and we went to the same table I'd earlier shared with Christine. Without a change of expression, the same waiter took our orders. We sat across from each other, saying nothing but harboring a multitude of thoughts.

"So," Jason said, breaking the silence, "I take it you didn't know that I even exist."

"That's correct," I said, "although there really isn't a reason for me to know. I knew your father had gotten married, but we really didn't keep up with each other socially. And I'm not that close to your stepmother—she *is* your stepmother?"

"She married my father. I believe that makes her my stepmother. Why would I lie about something like that?" he said. "Besides, you saw her reaction at seeing me. Total recognition."

"Not happy recognition, either, I'd say."

He gave a little snort. "Christine and I have never gotten along. I suppose she had reason not to like me. I saw through her the first time Dad introduced us." He lowered his voice and pretended to be his father: "Jason, I want you to meet the woman I love and who will be my wife." His laugh was almost a giggle. " 'She's a gold digger,' I told him. I'll never forget the expression on her face at that moment. She knew, absolutely knew, that I wasn't someone she could con. Ever have that experience, Mrs. Fletcher? You're talking to somebody, and you get a feeling they're a complete phony. And they know you aren't buying their act."

I simply nodded.

Our cups were placed on the table. Jason picked up his, extended it to me in what passed as a toast, and said, "Here's to literature." He took a sip. "And to the airline business."

I didn't raise my cup. I left it in its saucer and said, "You live here in London?"

He nodded. "Came here about eight years ago."

"To do what?"

A shrug accompanied his response. "To see what it was like. My mother was British."

"Oh? She was your father's first wife?"

"Actually, she was his second. He was married before that, but not for long. I think it lasted less than a year."

"They must have been very young."

"Yeah, they were." He drank a long sip. "They make good coffee here."

"They were divorced?"

"I guess so. I really don't know. You could never get a straight answer from my father."

"I never knew your mother," I said. "Wayne had left Cabot Cove, and nobody heard from him for a long time. I think perhaps that was when he was in Las Vegas."

"Yeah, I guess that's where he was."

"You didn't communicate?"

"No. Daddy was too busy making deals to keep in touch with me."

"Are you his only child?"

"That's me. His only heir."

Sitting there with this young man I'd just met had a surrealistic quality to it. As he relaxed, he became talkative. We chatted as though we were old friends who hadn't seen each other in a long time and were catching up on lost years. Yet he was someone who'd suddenly been reinjected into his stepmother's life in a decidedly unpleasant way. He was not fond of Christine—that was easy to see—and his tone said loud and clear that he wasn't a fan of his deceased father, either. He was willing to linger with me over a cup of coffee and happily answer my questions, none of which I had the right to ask. But as long as he was willing, I intended to keep posing them. I was naturally curious about him, of course. But significantly more important was that by showing up, he'd included himself in the mix of possible suspects.

"Do you have a relationship with your mother?" I asked.

"That'd be tough to do," he said. "She's dead."

"I'm sorry," I said.

"Yeah, she was murdered."

He said it so flatly, so without affect, that I was stunned.

"Did they apprehend her murderer?" I asked.

"The police? No. But somebody did."

"Who is that?"

"Whoever killed my father."

"What are you suggesting?"

"I'm suggesting, Mrs. Fletcher, that justice was finally done," he said. "My father killed my mother, and somebody killed him. Case closed."

He'd said it with finality and force, and had leaned

closer from the other side of the table to lock eyes with me, daring me to react. I met his stare. "That's a serious crime to accuse your father of," I said. "Do you have proof to back up your allegation? Or is this just a *feeling* you have?"

"Of course I don't have proof," he said. "If I did, he would be alive today, wouldn't he? Alive and rotting away in a jail cell." Jason sat back and crossed his long legs, a satisfied smile on his face. "I don't care whether you, or anyone else, believe me. I know it's true, and that's good enough for me."

"Did you ever confront your father about it?" I asked, now anxious to learn everything I could from him.

"Sure. That's when we parted company. He told me that he never again wanted to see a son who'd think such a thing." He guffawed. "Some defense, huh? He never flat-out denied it, never took the time or made the effort to prove to me that I was wrong. Just go away, was his message. He was a fraud, Mrs. Fletcher, and if you're looking for a sign from me that I'm sad that he was murdered, you're wasting your time."

"I don't expect anything from you, Jason. I've just met you. You're the one who's chosen to share your accusation with me." I waved off the waiter when he lifted the teapot to pour me another cup. "I assume you've seen the reports on television about your father's murder."

"And read the morning papers. That's how I know

I've become the owner of SilverAir. By the way, your picture looked good on the 'telly,' as the Brits call it. They have a silly name for everything."

"I imagine the question of ownership of your father's airline will be resolved by lawyers, Jason. I assume you have some legal proof to back up your claim."

He patted the breast pocket of his leather jacket. "Right here," he said.

When he didn't offer more information, I asked, "What is it?"

"You ask a lot of questions, don't you, Mrs. Fletcher?"

"You offer a lot of information, Jason."

He acknowledged my comment with a smirk. "And you like that."

"I find your sudden arrival interesting, that's all," I said, "particularly since it coincides with your father's murder."

He pulled his head back, his expression exaggerated shock. "Maybe I killed the old man. Is that what you're thinking?"

"Did you?"

"You've read too many of your own murder mysteries, Mrs. Fletcher."

"You didn't answer my question. Did you?" I repeated. "Kill your father? It certainly sounds as though you had a motive."

"Dream on, Mrs. Fletcher. I'd better get to my meeting."

"About the airline?"

"Right on. This was nice." He stood. "Thanks for

the coffee. Oh, and good luck solving Daddy's murder. They mentioned on the telly that you arrived at the scene with Scotland Yard. If nothing else, maybe you'll have a plot for your next book. Hope you don't mind my leaving you with the check. Don't have much pocket change at the moment. But that's bound to change, dontcha think? Cheerio, as the Limeys say. Don't forget your brolly if it rains."

He started to walk away, stopped, turned, and said, "And if you need a ladies' room, the loos are over there by the coat check."

I was perplexed, to say the least. Things were complex enough without having this cocksure young man, with an overt hatred of both his father and stepmother, show up unannounced and unexpected, claiming to own SilverAir. Did he really have legal documents that would give credence to his claim? His name never surfaced when I read about the airline before flying it to London at Wayne Silverton's invitation. There were a number of partners, with Mr. Casale and Mr. Vicks listed as major shareholders. There were a number of banks and investment companies also involved. Wayne was the largest stockholder, according to material issued by the company. *Jason Silverton?* Was he mentally unbalanced, fantasizing about being left the airline by his father? Judging from what he'd said, that was more than unlikely. They hadn't had contact with each other for years. *Or had they?* If so, Christine evidently didn't have any notion of it. *Or had she?* Had she been aware of the possibility that her husband's son by a previous marriage might emerge from what sounded like a life of exile, and claim a stake in SilverAir?

Those questions, however, paled in comparison to what Jason charged had caused his mother's demise. Surely, he was wrong. Could Wayne really have murdered his second wife, Jason's mother?

Families! No outsider can ever know for certain what goes on within any family, the tensions, rivalries, triumphs, and failures. Most families, at least the ones I know, seem to be solidly grounded and happy. But one can never be sure.

In the case of Silverton's family, there had obviously been a fermenting cauldron of distrust, and even hatred. So sad. Had Wayne Silverton not been slain, they would have gone on protecting their secrets and shielding their unhappiness from all but those most intimately involved with them.

But that didn't represent reality.

Wayne Silverton had been murdered.

Was the motive greed or jealousy or revenge? Caused by long-standing resentments, or a more recent business deal gone sour?

I knew one thing for certain. The plot had thickened, as happens in murder mystery novels, including my own. But this wasn't fiction.

This was as real as it got.

Chapter Thirteen

The first thing I did after signing the check was to call George on his cell phone.

"Is everything all right?" he asked.

I stepped through the door held open for me by a uniformed staff member, and walked down the sidewalk, out of earshot of those waiting in front of the hotel for a taxi. "Everything is fine, except I came upon a new wrinkle in the case I thought you should know about." I related my encounter with Jason Silverton.

"Well, well. You say he claims that he now owns the airline?"

"Yes."

"And that his father killed one of his former wives?"

"That's what he said."

"That's quite a development, indeed."

"I thought so, too."

"Does this young man strike you as someone with all his mental faculties?"

"You mean, do I think he's unbalanced?" I thought about Jason's demeanor during our time together. "It's hard to say. He's definitely having an emotional reaction to his father's death, mostly satisfaction. I can't be sure. I would need to spend a lot more time with him before I'd be willing to venture a guess on that. I did think it might be prudent, however, to see if he has a criminal record. He seems to have led an aimless life while here—he moved to London about eight years ago, according to him."

"Easy to do," George said. "I'll run a check on him immediately."

"Good. I can tell you Christine was stunned when he arrived."

"On top of her previous shock. How does she appear to be holding up?"

"Well, I think. She's a strong lady. She's immersed in discussions regarding the restructuring of Silver-Air now that Wayne is gone."

"Should be a fascinating series of meetings," he said with a chuckle.

"To say the least. Are we still on with Captain Caine at eleven?"

"Oh, yes. I might get there even earlier than anticipated. I'll ring your room."

"Or have me paged."

"Till later, then. See you at eleven," he said, and clicked off.

I closed the cell phone, replaced it in my handbag, and stood on the sidewalk, thinking.

A deep voice interrupted my reverie. "Those look like very serious thoughts."

I looked up to see Jed Richardson coming toward me.

"Good morning, Jessica. Am I interrupting? Are you solving the problems of the world?"

"Good morning, Jed. Nothing quite so momentous. All set for a pleasant day in London? The weather is cooperating."

"Yes. I've hooked up with an old friend from my airline days. We're having lunch at Heathrow."

"Sounds like fun. Have you had a chance to chat with Captain Caine since we arrived?"

"No. He's stayed pretty much to himself." He lowered his voice. "I did hear him the other night, though."

"Hear him?"

"Yeah. My room's across the hall from his. He got into a shouting match that was pretty heated."

"Was it with the flight attendant? Gina Molnari?"

"No, actually, I believe it was a man. In fact, I thought he was yelling at his first officer."

"Oh my. Could you tell what they were arguing about?"

"I don't know, Jess. I did listen for a while, but I

never made out their words, just an occasional one now and then. That's how I know it was the first officer in the room with him. I heard him say, 'Cut it out, Carl.' And later I thought I heard Caine call him 'Scherer' once."

I lightened my voice as I said, "Somehow, having the captain and first officer fighting doesn't bode well for the flight home."

"They'll get over it," Jed said. "I've had my share of disagreements with first officers when I was flying commercial, but it never lasted. Too much at stake once you're in that cockpit. Speaking of cockpits, how did you enjoy your ride up front?"

"Loved it, of course."

"I thought you might grab an hour of dual piloting instruction while here, you know, get a taste of how the British general aviation system works."

"No time for that," I said. "Enjoy your lunch with your friend. We'll catch up later."

"Shall do. By the way, that flight attendant you mentioned. Isn't she the one who tried to take her life? She okay now?"

"I haven't heard anything," I said. "She evidently wasn't in any danger. I suppose she's staying in her room, embarrassed about what she did."

"She shouldn't be," he said. "I just hope she's all right."

"I'm sure she's fine. Jed, before you go, is there some way that you can check on the background of Captain Caine and First Officer Scherer?"

"Background?"

"In aviation. I'm just curious how they ended up flying for SilverAir, what other airlines they worked for, things like that."

"Sure. I can ask around. Where will you be this afternoon?"

"Not sure, but I'll be here somewhere. The limos pick us up at the hotel at seven for the flight back."

"We'll catch up," he said. "Have a good one."

I wandered back into the hotel, debating whether I needed to change clothes before taking the walk I'd promised myself earlier. But the decision was made for me. Churlson Vicks, Wayne's British partner in SilverAir, called my name as he closed the gap between us with long, purposeful strides.

"Good morning, Mr. Vicks."

"Not a very good morning, I'd say," he said. Although he was a man who obviously maintained control of himself in stressful situations, he demonstrated exasperation.

"I'm sorry to hear that," I said.

"The question is," he said, "what part do you play in this circus?"

"Pardon?"

"This perversion, this—" He realized he was sputtering, and forced calm into his voice. "Silverton's kid," he said.

"Jason?"

"You *are* involved."

"Involved in what?"

"This travesty, this, this—"

His control was ebbing again.

"Mr. Vicks, I assume you're talking about Wayne's son showing up and claiming he now owns at least a part of the airline. But why you would accuse me of being involved is beyond my comprehension."

"That young rotter has some bloody nerve. How dare he come in here and claim he owns anything? He said he'd been meeting with you."

"That's absurd. I was standing with Christine when he arrived unexpectedly. She walked away, and he and I had a cup of tea together. Coffee, actually, for him. He indicated to me that he had papers of some sort that entitled him to ownership of Silver-Air. That's all I know. But to claim we had a meeting is preposterous."

"No surprise, coming from the likes of him. Nothing but a young hooligan, a grifter if I've ever seen one."

"I wouldn't know about that, Mr. Vicks. The question is, does he have some sort of legally binding paper that substantiates his claim?"

A derisive laugh exploded from his lips. "So he says," he said. "He presented us with what he claims is proof that his departed father left him his share of the airline. Pure rubbish! It's a letter his father had written him years ago—many years ago—saying in it that he one day intended to launch a new airline, and that he would be pleased to have his only son as his partner. Balderdash! A worthless scrap of paper if I've ever seen one."

"But does it have validity?" I pressed.

"The lawyers are looking it over as we speak. I apologize for accusing you of being in cahoots with him, Mrs. Fletcher. Frankly, if I were that despicable young man, I'd be in fear of my life."

"That's a harsh statement," I said.

"Not if you know Sal."

"Mr. Casale?"

"Did you read about his goons being arrested last night?"

"I read about two men being arrested at the airport. Are you suggesting that—?"

"I'm suggesting nothing. But the next time you have tea, or coffee, with Mr. Jason Silverton, you might do him a bloody favor and tell him he'd best disappear again or face the consequences."

I wanted to ask about Christine, whether she, too, had laid a claim to a piece of SilverAir, and what her response had been to her stepson's rival claim, but Vicks walked away before I could.

I visited the ladies' room off the lobby, my multiple cups of tea taking their toll, then hurried from the hotel lobby to the Strand, and set out on my walk before I could be waylaid by anyone else. I turned left and walked toward Charing Cross Station. When it opened in 1864, Charing Cross turned the Strand into Europe's busiest street, replete with lavish hotels, majestic theaters, and many restaurants. The Strand is no longer the posh thoroughfare it once was, but a sense of history prevails, as it does on virtually every street in London. As I walked, I could almost feel and see those literary giants whose footsteps preceded mine on this celebrated section of the city: Samuel Johnson, James Boswell, Charles Lamb, William Thackeray, and Charles Dickens, among dozens of other great names from a bygone era. I looked down Craven Street, where Benjamin Franklin lived during two extended stays in London, and paused in front of the magnificent Adelphi Theatre, built by a wealthy tradesman to launch his daughter's acting career, and the scene of an infamous shooting of the actor William Terris by a madman. And another theater caught my attention, the Vaudeville, dating from 1870. A complete restoration in the 1960s turned it into one of the city's nicest theaters; I've enjoyed more than one production in its elegant surroundings.

I walked as far as the station; then, refreshed in body and spirit, I returned to the Savoy and went to my room. The message light was flashing on my telephone. I retrieved two messages. One was from Seth, informing me that he wouldn't be at lunch. He'd made contact with the British physician who'd been summoned to the Savoy to minister to Gina Molnari, and had been invited to spend time with him at the hospital where he was affiliated. I wasn't surprised. Seth often does that, befriending doctors from different places and learning how they conduct their practices. The United Kingdom, of course, has socialized medicine, vastly different from our health care system. I'd be interested in Seth's reaction to being exposed to the British version.

The second call was from George. He said he was heading for the hotel and would be there by ten thirty. I looked at my watch. It was almost that time now.

I freshened up and was waiting when he called the room.

"Tea?" he asked.

"I've had my fill of tea for one day," I said, pleasantly. "But I'd be happy to meet you downstairs."

We found a small couch in a secluded corner of the large, ornate lobby. He handed me a computer printout of Jason Silverton's rap sheet. I took a quick look. "Whew," I said. "Hardly an upstanding citizen."

"Not as bad as some, but bad enough."

According to the printout, Jason had been arrested six times since arriving in London. Two of the offenses were domestic battery.

"He's been married?" I asked.

"No," George replied. "That code there indicates he battered two live-ins, significant others I suppose you call them, although judging from his behavior, one would have to question just how significant they were."

"What does this code mean?" I asked.

"The one charge was dropped when the victim declined to press charges. In the other case, he pleaded no contest and received probation."

"Fraud?" I said, referring to another entry on the sheet.

"Yes. I went back into the files to learn a little more about his two fraud cases. It seems he tried to sell what he purported were rare, first-edition copies of books. He evidently was a good salesman. His pigeons bought, discovered they'd been had, and brought suits against him."

"Criminal suits."

"Criminal and civil. As you can see, he was found not guilty of both charges."

"He's done quite well in your courts."

"Not always. These final two charges didn't pan out quite as nicely for him. See there? Six months for burglary, and—"

"And a year and a half for impersonation for the purpose of fraud," I said.

We looked at each other.

I shook my head. "No, George, he must be Wayne Silverton's son. Christine didn't question it for a moment."

"I'm sure you're right, Jessica. But that doesn't mean he's above forging documents to back up his claim about the airline. You haven't seen those papers?"

"No, I haven't." I told him of my conversation

with Churlson Vicks about Jason's presence in the meeting. "Just an old letter from his father."

"If he's trying to pull wool over the eyes of those sharks, he'll find himself in rather dangerous waters," George said.

"I'm sure the attorneys involved will vet that letter thoroughly to ascertain its legitimacy," I said.

"For his sake, let's hope so." George looked at his watch. "Time to see the good Captain Caine. You've met him a few times now. What's your evaluation of the man?"

"Our encounters have been relatively short," I said. "I sat in the cockpit on takeoff from Boston. It was a thrill. As for Captain Caine, he seemed to me to be a no-nonsense sort of fellow, very much the professional airline pilot. He wasn't especially happy to have me in the cockpit, but Wayne arranged it. And the captain took it in his stride. That reminds me. I haven't told you about the confrontation that occurred between Wayne and the captain."

"About what?"

"About Caine's decision to leave the lineup of planes waiting to take off, and return to the terminal to have a possible malfunction checked."

"What was the problem?"

"A lightbulb, it turned out, but of course he didn't know that at the time. Captain Caine made a decision to return to the gate. Wayne wanted Caine to ignore the problem and take off. In the end, there was nothing seriously wrong, but I admired the captain's stand. Wayne was out of line to try to override Caine's decision by throwing around his weight as the airline owner."

"Sounds like Silverton was adept at making enemies. What do you say about Ms. Molnari taking the pills in Caine's room? Any significance?"

"Only the obvious. We should ask him if they've ever been romantically involved. I happened to speak with someone this morning who has a room across the hall from Caine. Jed Richardson. He's Cabot Cove's resident pilot. In fact, he taught me to fly. He told me he'd heard an argument between Captain Caine and another man. He's pretty sure it was the first officer, Carl Scherer."

"And?"

"Nothing beyond that. But I asked him if he could check on the captain's and first officer's professional backgrounds. Jed used to be a commercial pilot. He knows whom to ask."

George smiled. "You've had a busy morning, I see. By the way, I managed to spend an unplanned fifteen minutes with the first officer, Mr. Scherer. Pleasant enough young chap."

"Did anything come of it?"

"No, nor did I expect anything. Just an informal chat. He offered to sit down for a longer interview with me at my convenience. He rode the limousine into London with the rest of the flight crew."

"Did he have anything to offer regarding the murder?"

"No. He spoke highly of Mr. Silverton, called him an aviation visionary."

"Which I suppose he was."

"At any rate, Jessica, Mr. Scherer strikes me as a forthright fellow. I'll find the time to follow up with him as soon as possible."

George stood and put out his hand to help me up. "Shall we?"

As we headed for the elevators, George nodded at a man in the lobby—a plain clothes officer, I suspected. "It should be interesting," he said in a low voice, "to see how the captain responds to the news that his fingerprints are all over the knife used in the murder."

My wonderful British friend is a master of understatement.

Chapter Fourteen

Captain Caine answered George's knock.

"Good morning, Captain."

"Good morning." Caine looked past George to me, and his eyes widened. "How are you, Mrs. Fletcher?"

"Just fine, thank you."

"May we come in?" George asked.

"Yeah, sure."

We entered his suite where Gina Molnari sat stiffly in a chair by the window. She turned at our entrance but said nothing.

"Ms. Molnari," George said, cocking his head, "I trust you're feeling better."

"I'm fine," she said.

She didn't look fine to me. There were dark circles under her eyes, and her face was puffy and pale.

George said to Caine, "I'd prefer that we speak alone, Captain."

"Anything I have to say, she already knows," Caine replied.

"That may be," George said, "but I insist that this interview be conducted without anyone else present."

"What about her?" Caine asked, indicating me.

"I've asked Mrs. Fletcher to accompany me on some of my interviews. She's been involved from the beginning, and I find her insights to be useful."

"Her imagination, you mean," Caine said.

"I beg your pardon?" George's voice was cold.

Caine hesitated, looking unsure that he wanted to challenge George. "She's a novelist," he said after a moment. "She makes up stories. That's what I meant."

"Be that as it may," George said, "Ms. Molnari will have to leave and Mrs. Fletcher stays."

Caine started to protest again, but Gina stood. "I'll be in my room," she said, and left without another word.

"Have a seat," George said to Caine. The pilot was dressed in a gray sweatshirt, tan cargo shorts, and sneakers sans socks. George and I took the couch, Caine a chair across a coffee table from us. George took out his notebook and placed it carefully on the table.

"Let me save you some time," Caine said. "I don't know why that knife is missing from my carry-on bag. Chances are I left it at home, forgot to pack it."

George had been bent over the tabletop, his eyes on his notebook. Without moving his head, he looked up from beneath his thick eyebrows. "I believe you said it stays in your bag all the time," he said.

"It usually does. This time it didn't," Caine said. He tapped his heel on the floor, causing his knee to bounce up and down. "If you're trying to link up my missing knife with Silverton's murder, you're wasting your time."

George reached out a hand and rested it on top of his notebook. "I'm afraid it's not quite that simple, Captain. You see, the knife that killed Mr. Silverton has your fingerprints on it. Now, if the murder weapon is not your knife, how did it get your fingerprints all over it? That would point to you as the murderer, would it not?"

"I don't believe this," said Caine, running his fingers through his hair. "I'm telling you I didn't kill him. But what does it matter? Somebody took the knife from my bag and stabbed Silverton. It doesn't take a genius to figure that out."

"That's certainly a possibility," George said. "Who had access to your bag aside from you?"

Caine snorted, "Hell, anyone and everyone. The crew—Carl Scherer, the flight attendants—and dozens of people in Ops at Logan and Stansted, the world." He looked at me. "You spent time up front with us, Mrs. Fletcher. The bag was right there at your feet, just off to the left of the jump seat you used."

"Yes, I remember seeing it," I said, "but I wouldn't have had any reason to open it and rummage through its contents."

"I'm not saying you did," Caine said, "but it makes my point. Everybody on the flight had an opportunity to grab the knife from it. Scherer and I left the cockpit after we'd landed and shut down. The door was open. This wasn't like a normal flight where security was tight. Hell, there wasn't any security. Silverton saw to that. He didn't want to 'offend' anyone." He delivered that last line scornfully.

George's index finger tapped the notebook. "Thank you for sharing that information with us," he said. "Would you mind accounting for your movements from the time you landed the plane at Stansted until later that night?" He drew a pen from his breast pocket, opened the notebook, and looked at Caine expectantly.

"Let's see," Caine said, his expression announcing that he was thinking, his knee keeping time to some internal music. "I did the postflight rundown, went to Ops, and closed out the flight plan. There's always a lot of paperwork. And then—then I came into town along with everyone else."

"No, you didn't," I said.

His face turned angry. "What?"

"I said you didn't come into town with the others. I saw you at the airport when Inspector Sutherland and I went there after being notified about Mr. Silverton's death."

George deliberately flipped back a few pages in his notebook. "And I have several witnesses who say you didn't take the crew limo into London," he added.

The captain squirmed a bit, readjusting his position

in the chair so he was leaning forward, his elbow on his now-still knee. He shrugged. "I didn't say I came into London right away. Truth is, I did, um, I did stay out at the airport for a while."

"Why?" I asked, not sure if I should have injected myself into the questioning. I glanced at George, whose face said I was on solid ground.

Caine sat back. "You're too nosey for my taste, Mrs. Fletcher."

"I've heard that before," I said. "Are you trying to avoid my question?"

He glared at George. "I don't see why I have to answer questions from her. She's not a cop."

George's expression remained neutral. "Answer the question, please."

"I don't even remember it."

"Why didn't you come into London with the rest of the crew?" I asked.

His laugh wasn't genuine. "All right," he said, "let me satisfy that nose of yours." His knee started to bounce again. "I was about to take the limo when I bumped into an old pal. We used to fly for the same airline. He'd just arrived at Stansted, too, so we decided to grab a beer together. Simple as that."

"At the airport?" George asked.

"A local pub."

"Name of the pub?"

Caine rolled his shoulders. "Let me see. I think it was called the Rose and Crown. Nice place, friendly people, and the beer on tap was good," he said with a tight smile.

"Do you think people would remember you there?" George asked.

"Do you mean did I make a scene, spill my beer on somebody, get into a brawl? No. We sat at a quiet table far from the crowd and were perfect gentlemen. Unless, of course, the sizable tip I left the barmaid is remembered. Hell, it should be."

"Captain Caine," I said, "At the risk of offending you again, I'd like to ask if that was a wise decision."

"Huh? Leaving a big tip? What's wrong with that?"

"You mistake my meaning. I thought there were restrictions on pilots drinking."

"Oh, very good, Mrs. Fletcher. You're right. The regs against consuming alcoholic beverages before a flight are strict. Fact is, I knew I had this layover in London. The rules say no drinking for twenty-four hours before flying. I had more time than that before we were scheduled to fly back to Boston. So I had a beer."

"What about your friend?" George asked.

"Lemonade, if I remember correctly. No alcohol in that. They also have what's called a shandy here in the UK, Mrs. Fletcher, half beer, half lemonade. There's always plenty of lemonade at pubs." He looked at George. "But you must know that."

"I've enjoyed a shandy or two," George said.

"I don't know how anyone drinks it," Caine said. "They say it lets you stay longer at the bar without getting drunk. I'd rather get drunk than drink that stuff."

George ignored Caine's review of local customs and said, "I'm sure you don't mind giving us your chum's name." His pen was poised over the small notebook.

Caine obliged. "He's based in San Francisco," he added.

"Why did you return to the airport?" I asked.

"Nothing nefarious. My buddy left his keys at Ops. I went back with him to collect them. I saw this whole commotion, and I didn't stick around to see what it was about. That good enough for you?"

"Thank you," George said. "Now, back to the business of your knife being the one used to kill Mr. Silverton, the one with your prints on it. I assume you could identify the knife as belonging to you."

"Don't count on it," Caine said. "I know what my knife looked like. It's a plain and simple folding knife, nothing special. There must be a million like it. I'd never be able to swear it was mine."

"No identifying marks on it, no nicks in the blade that you're aware of?" George asked.

"Who knows? I haven't looked at it in months."

A lull in the conversation descended on the room. I broke it with, "Was Ms. Molnari with you when you met your friend for a drink at the pub?"

"Gina? No. Why?"

"She didn't come into London in the crew limo, either," I explained.

"That's news to me," Caine said. "Why don't you ask her?"

"I'm sure Inspector Sutherland intends to do just that," I said.

As I spoke, a bolt of lightning lit up the sky outside the window, so vivid and electrifying that it seemed aimed directly at us. It was followed by a resounding clap of thunder that caused everyone in the room to flinch.

"There's a series of fronts coming through over the next twenty-four hours," Caine said. "Severe thunderstorms, hail, the works. Supposed to arrive tonight. Looks like it's getting here a little early."

"Will it change our flight plans?" I asked.

Caine relaxed at the easy question. "Incoming flights will be affected, but we should be okay. Anything else you want to ask?"

George shook his head, and looked to me.

"I do have one other question," I said.

"Shoot," Caine said.

"Did the sleeping pills Ms. Molnari took belong to you?"

"You already asked me that. I told you they didn't."

"Did she bring them into the room with her?"

"I would have to assume she did. I don't use sleeping pills."

"Did you see her take them?"

"I saw the results of it. That's why I called for a doctor."

"Do you know where she got them?"

"How would I know that?"

"They were a prescription," I said.

"And?"

"And—the prescription was in the name of Christine Silverton."

"I don't see why that should mean anything to me," Caine said.

"It probably shouldn't," I said with a smile. "Thank you for allowing me to get a few things off my chest."

He rose from his chair. "Anytime for a fellow pilot. Happy to have you back up front when we leave tonight."

"I look forward to it."

We expressed our appreciation for the captain's time and left his suite. As we approached the elevators, I opened the door to the stairwell. "Are we walking downstairs," George asked.

"Let's stand in here for a moment," I said.

"Why?" he asked as he joined me. I left the door slightly ajar, just enough to afford a view of the long hallway from that vantage point. As I expected, Captain Caine came from his room, went to Ms. Molnari's door, and knocked. It opened, and he disappeared inside.

"I imagine they have a lot to talk about," I said,

exiting the stairwell and pressing the button for the elevator.

"I'm sure you're right," George agreed. "Ah, to be the proverbial fly on the wall."

We rode down in silence and I accompanied him as he left the Savoy through the main doors.

"You're off to your luncheon at the Grenadier," he said.

"Yes. Sure you won't join us?"

"Positive. I have a lot of paperwork to push through before our three o'clock talk with Mrs. Silverton."

He kissed my cheek and walked away. We don't often think of law enforcement officers as being especially sensitive. They spend their days and nights dealing with the unpleasant aspects of the human condition, the cruel and wanton disregard for life by criminals, the heartbreak and sorrow of people caught in tough circumstances, many times not of their own doing. But there are numerous exceptions, of course. George Sutherland certainly ranked at the top of that list.

As I returned to my room to prepare to go to lunch, I thought of George's late wife, who'd died of cancer. He'd had little to say about her—her name was Elizabeth—except that she was a wonderful woman who'd left this world far too soon. Once, when we were sitting on a park bench in London, he'd showed me a picture of her. She was lovely, a raven-haired Scottish beauty with dark, soulful eyes, and a hint of merriment on her lips. I spoke on that day of my late husband, Frank, a fine, fun-loving man whose life had also been cut short prematurely. I tried to shift mental gears and not think about George as I changed into another outfit, but was only partially successful. My skills at keeping personal thoughts separate from investigative analysis were not as well-honed as my handsome inspector's.

By the time I came to the Savoy's entrance and waited for a doorman to put me in one of those heavenly London taxicabs, I'd managed to turn my focus on that morning's events—and there was plenty to chew on. The rain was coming down hard, sheets of water at times, and getting to the pub was a slow process. But we finally arrived. I paid the driver, a courteous older gentleman who wished me a splendid day despite the weather—"Good for the pretty flowers, ma'am"—put up my umbrella, and hurried past the bright red sentry box and through the door of the red, white, and blue pub on Wilton Row. I don't like being late—for anything. People who are perpetually late smack of arrogance and ego, always making their grand entrance while others wait in anticipation. But because my reputation is that of one who is seldom behind schedule, being a few minutes late didn't seem to be noticed or commented upon.

"How was your morning?" Mort asked once I'd been seated and had a tall glass of Bloody Mary mix in front of me, minus the vodka. They call such a drink in England a "Bloody Shame," the name stemming from deeply religious waiters and waitresses balking at having to order "Virgin Marys" from bartenders.

We were in one of two small rooms at the rear of the pub, the walls paneled in dark wood, the ceiling coffee black. The walls were covered with military memorabilia, lethal-looking bayonets and sabers, breastplates, and bearskins. No doubt about it, this historic pub had plenty of history behind it, including its infamous, card-cheating ghost.

"Fine," I answered. "All of you?"

"We had a great time," Susan Shevlin said. "Those soldiers standing at attention are so impressive. I don't know how they can do it, not move a muscle while thousands of tourists like us gawk at them and take their pictures."

"Just a matter of discipline," Mort offered.

"You try it," said Jim Shevlin. "I give you ten minutes before you pass out."

"I don't know. If I had the right training, I might be able to do it." He turned to me. "So, Mrs. F., tell us what's new and exciting with the murder?"

"Mort! We're supposed to be on vacation," Maureen said. "You promised me you wouldn't get involved."

"I'm just asking a question, Hon. That's not getting involved."

"You can take the man away from his job," said Jim, "but you can't take the policeman out of the man, or something like that."

Susan groaned.

We all laughed at Jim's bungled analogy.

"Thanks, Mayor," Mort said, and smiled at his wife.

Maureen shrugged and said, "Sorry, Jessica."

"No need to be," I said.

"Go on. Give us an update," she said.

"The case becomes more tangled with each passing hour," I said. "George and I interviewed Captain Caine this morning."

"*You* and the inspector?" Jim said. "How did *you* end up in that situation?"

"George feels that—well, because I was with him the night we went to the airport after he'd been notified of Wayne's murder—well, he feels that I can be of some help in the investigation."

"It's not the first time you've been in that situation," Maureen said. "I remember when—"

"Please," I said, "let's not rehash those unfortunate situations. The truth is, George feels that because I'm part of the inner circle, so to speak, as one of the passengers familiar with others on the trip, that I might have insights to contribute that he would miss as an outsider."

"Makes sense to me," Mort said. "You've been plenty helpful to me, Mrs. F., back in Cabot Cove, when I've had a murder on my hands."

"And you were a dear to let me poke my nose in," I said, patting his arm. "Since you're all likely to meet him at some point, I should mention that Wayne has a son from a previous marriage. Did anyone know that?" I looked from face to face, but the blank expressions confirmed my suspicion that Jason's existence was not something Wayne ever discussed. At least, it had never reached the Cabot Cove grapevine—and that's a powerful source of information.

"He claims that his father left him his stake in SilverAir."

Now there were overt expressions of interest on everyone's part.

"Is it true?" Maureen asked.

"I have no idea," I said, opening my menu. "I do know that I'm hungry."

We enjoyed standard pub fare prepared with a deft hand in the kitchen. Mort insisted that we all taste one of the pub's featured beers, "bitter" as it's called, and we did. I'm not a beer lover, although there are certain days in the heat of summer back home when a frosty glass of beer hits the spot the way no other cold drink can. The beer at the Grenadier was tasty, but I drank only a third of mine. Mort might not have been participating in the investigation, but I was, and I wanted to be as mentally sharp as possible for the rest of the day.

"I hope this weather doesn't delay the flight tonight," Maureen said as she left the table in search of the ladies' room.

"I spoke with Captain Caine about that this morning," I told the others. "He said that incoming flights might be delayed, but departures should be all right."

"What's on your agenda for the rest of the afternoon, Mrs. F.?" Mort asked, obviously straining a bit at the restrictions he had agreed to.

I had the three o'clock interview with Christine Silverton, but didn't mention it. Instead, I said, "I thought I'd hibernate in my suite and do some reading."

It wasn't a lie. I'd decided during the taxi ride to the pub to do just that, sandwiching the meeting with Christine in between chapters of *The French Girls of Kilini*, a book of stories written years ago by Arturo Vivante, one of my favorite authors. I've read it at least a dozen times and never tire of it.

"What's keeping Maureen?" Mort asked, looking in the direction she'd gone. Suddenly, she appeared, shock and fear written all over her ghostly pale face.

"What's wrong, Hon?" Mort asked, helping her into the chair.

"I saw him," she managed.

"Saw whom?" Jim asked.

"The soldier. The one who was flogged to death here." She wrapped her arms about herself and began to shake.

There was some nervous laughter.

"I did!" she said. "I was coming out of the ladies'

room and almost bumped into him. He was wearing his uniform, and his face was streaked with blood. He looked horrible."

"Did he say or do anything?" I asked.

"He was gone, poof, just like that," she said, now under better control of herself. She smiled weakly. "I know it sounds silly, but—"

"Nonsense," I said. "If you say you saw him, then that's what you did. Come on, time to go."

As we passed through the pub room where dozens of people were lined up along the length of the pewter bar top, I stayed back and motioned for the bartender, a large, red-faced gentleman with an outgoing disposition.

"Yes, ma'am?" he said.

"One of my friends went to the loo. When she came out, she's convinced she saw the soldier who'd allegedly been flogged to death in this pub."

He let out a deep, rumbling laugh. "Of course she saw him, ma'am. He's always here but decides to show himself only now and then. Seen him dozens of times myself. He's fussy about who he shows himself to. She should be honored."

"Thank you," I said, and joined the others outside where the rain hadn't let up a bit. There wasn't a cab in sight, but everyone had been smart enough to bring along an umbrella, and we set out with them raised, not minding getting our feet wet and enjoying the exercise after a substantial meal. Eventually we found a taxi and the five of us settled into the cab's roomy back, happy to be together but each undoubtedly engaged in thoughts not quite so pleasant.

Mort wasn't the only one interested in the investigation. Wayne Silverton's murder was understandably on everyone's mind, imagined visions of what he must have looked like (I didn't have to use my imagination, of course), speculating on how it happened and whether he was aware that he was about to be stabbed. If so, what ran through his mind the few seconds before the actual act? Did he sense it coming? Did he feel pain, or had the initial thrust of the knife severed a nerve that precluded his feeling anything?

The cockpit was too small, too cramped for someone to be able to enter unannounced. Wayne must have known his assailant, I thought. From what I'd seen in the cockpit that night, he hadn't put up a fight, hadn't raised his hands in self-defense. They were on the thrust levers. He fell forward when he was stabbed, his body pushing the control yoke, his hands doing the same with the levers.

Perhaps his killer had been in the cockpit for a period of time, however brief, prior to committing the act, which meant Wayne knew that the person was there, possibly welcoming his or her presence.

It was all well and good to conjure what the scene was like.

The more important question: Who was in the cockpit with him, the last person to see him alive?

"Jess," Maureen said once we were inside the Savoy.

"Yes, Maureen?"

"You believe me, don't you?"

"Of course I do." I made a point of leaning close to her ear and speaking in a low, conspiratorial tone. "I asked the bartender about the ghost."

"You did?"

"Yes. And he swears he's seen him, too, many times. He says it's an honor. The ghost is very finicky about whom he reveals himself to."

"I could have done without that particular honor," Maureen said with a shiver.

"I think I would like to have seen him," I said, smiling.

She returned my smile. "Thank you, Jess."

"My pleasure, Maureen."

The return trip had taken longer than I had intended, leaving me with little time to enjoy reading. I'd just hung up my raincoat and taken out my book when George called.

"I know I'm early," he said.

"I'll be right down."

He was in the lobby, talking with a hotel employee, when I stepped off the elevator. I paused before going to him, taking a few seconds to simply observe the man. He wore his usual tweed jacket, blue button-down shirt, sharply creased tan slacks, and polished ankle-high boots, but it wasn't his attire that I admired at that moment. It was the way he stood, slightly stooped as tall men often are from a lifetime of ducking low objects. He was listening intently to what the hotel staffer was saying, another admirable trait. He gave the same concentrated attention conversing with a porter or cleaning woman as he did with a head of state. He's a superb listener, always more interested in what you were saying than in what he might have on his mind. His pose was relaxed, a man comfortable with himself.

I closed my eyes for a moment, drew a breath, and joined them.

After a cursory bow to me, the employee walked away.

"Interesting chap," George said. "Works maintenance here at the hotel, but collects rare musical memorabilia in his off time."

"I'm not at all surprised that you learned that about him. How long had you been talking?"

"Five minutes or so. How was your lunch?"

"It was fun. They're such good people, easy to be with. Did you get to eat?"

"A quick bite at the office." He turned and looked through the main doors. "That's one nasty day out there. Well, Jessica, ready for our chat with Mrs. Silverton?"

"I think so. Before we do, though, I've been thinking about the time we spent this morning with Captain Caine."

"So have I."

"I think he was lying when he said he wasn't

aware that Gina Molnari hadn't come into London with the rest of the crew."

"Why do you say that?"

"Intuition."

"That famed women's intuition?"

"I don't know whether it has anything to do with my gender, George, but I'm convinced that he and Ms. Molnari are romantically involved. All the signs are there."

"I'm quite sure you're right. But how does that tie in with the murder of Silverton?"

I laughed. "I haven't the slightest idea, George. I'm good at tossing out questions, less good at answering them. Let's see if Christine Silverton can shed some light."

Christine was not alone. She introduced the man in the suite as her attorney, Steven Bellnap.

"Mr. Bellnap flew to London this morning," she said after she'd invited us in, and we'd taken seats around a dining table adjacent to a Pullman kitchen.

"I'm here at Mrs. Silverton's request," he said.

"I imagine you've come to help sort out the business side of Mr. Silverton's untimely death," I said.

"That, among other things. I understand, Inspector Sutherland, that you're the lead investigator on the case."

"Yes, sir, that's true."

"And that Mrs. Fletcher is sort of—well, how shall I say it?—she's an unofficial part of your team?"

"You might say that," George responded.

"I'm also here to represent Mrs. Silverton in any criminal aspects of your investigation. I understand, of course, that everyone who accompanied Mr. Silverton on the flight must be considered a suspect, including Mrs. Silverton."

George didn't deny it. "A victim's spouse is always among the first people we look at." He peered into Christine's eyes as he said, "Your cooperation will go a long way toward allaying our suspicions."

"I'll do my best to answer your questions," she said.

"Provided that your questions remain focused on what's pertinent," Bellnap added.

While George and Bellnap talked, I took the opportunity to take a closer look at the attorney. He was probably in his midforties, although I've never been an especially good judge of other people's ages. He was nicely dressed. His lank brown hair had begun to leave him, and years of poring over legal briefs and other documents must have taken its toll on his eyesight. The lenses of his glasses were unusually thick. I decided on the spot that he was all business, a man with a thwarted sense of humor. Not that I intended to crack any jokes, but my summation of him would be helpful in how I approached my part of the meeting.

"Are you working in concert with a barrister here in the UK, Mr. Bellnap?" George asked.

"My firm has an affiliate here," he replied.

"Good," George said. He said to Christine, "I realize this may be uncomfortable for you, Mrs. Silverton, but I'm sure you understand the necessity
of it."

"Of course I do," she said, "although I don't see
why Jessica needs to be a part of it."

"Her presence is required," George said.

Bellnap frowned. "By whom?"

"By me," George said in a tone that ended any
debate. "Now, Mrs. Silverton, you obviously knew
your husband best. I'd like you to think back. What
was his mood prior to the flight? Was there anything,
either voiced or in his deportment, that indicated he
felt that his life was in danger?"

"No. Wayne had business enemies, of course. We
both knew that. But to suspect someone was out to
kill him? Absolutely not."

"Had he been acting out of sorts lately, changed
his usual patterns of behavior or activities?"

She shook her head. "He was excited about the
flight, and maybe a bit concerned about everything
being perfect. Wayne was very demanding of his
staff. He wanted everything perfectly planned and
perfectly executed. I imagine all CEOs are the same
way."

"I imagine so. And did he demand perfection in
you as well?"

Christine glanced nervously at me. "I'm not sure
I understand."

"Your marriage, Mrs. Silverton. I know this is sensitive, but I must ask it. Would you consider your marriage a happy one?"

Christine cleared her throat. "Yes, it was, Inspector. Wayne was devoted to me and I to him. We were very much in love. We were not only partners as man and wife, we were partners in SilverAir. We did everything together. His loss will be a deep and lasting tragedy for me."

Except you said Wayne cheated on you, I thought.

"I see," said George. "Let's go to the night in question, if you don't mind. When did you last see your husband?"

"On the flight, of course."

"And once you'd landed? He obviously stayed at Stansted after most of the others had left. When did you last speak with him?"

She sighed, evidently eager for this to be over.

"Wayne and I intended to come into London together. As I was ready to leave the aircraft, he said he had business to attend to at the airport and would join me later at the hotel."

"Did he say what sort of business?" George asked.

She laughed. "As you said, Inspector, I knew my husband quite well. I'm sure the so-called business was nothing more than wanting to hang around the aircraft, get in the cockpit, and pretend he was flying it. He was an inveterate dreamer."

"A nice thing to be," I said.

"Unless you carry it too far," Christine said. "Next question?"

"Was anyone else aboard the aircraft at that time?"

"I didn't see anyone."

"So," George said, "he was alive when you left him on the plane and came into London with the others."

"Correct."

George paused; I knew what he was about to ask next.

"Did you return to the airport after arriving at the Savoy?"

"Of course not. Why would I do that?"

Possibly to kill your husband, I thought.

"Mrs. Fletcher noticed something in your suite at the Savoy that would seem to suggest otherwise."

"Oh? What's that? I wasn't aware you were spying on me, Jessica?"

"You know I wasn't, Christine. We'd come up to tell you about Wayne."

Christine's voice was chilly. "So what was it that you found so interesting that you had to mention it to the inspector?"

"It may sound silly," I said, "but I noticed that your raincoat was damp."

"It was, after all, a rainy night," she said.

"More a misty one," I said. "At the airport, you got into the limousine, and when we arrived at the Savoy, we were sheltered by the overhang. I just wondered whether you'd gone back out in the mist."

"Well, the answer is no."

"And I also saw that your luggage hadn't been unpacked."

"So?"

"Oh, I don't know," I said, "but I remember talking with you once about that public relations program you'd launched when you were working as a flight attendant, the one where you gave talks at local civic and fraternal organizations about how to pack a bag."

She stared at me blankly.

"You made a point that savvy airline passengers always unpack the minute they get to the room, hanging up clothes to get the wrinkles out. I remember it well because it's something I've been doing my entire traveling life."

"As I recall, Jessica, I also said that the first thing every veteran traveler packs is plastic bags of assorted sizes. Can you find something ominous in that?"

"Of course not," I said with a smile. "Why didn't you unpack when you arrived in the room? When we saw you, it was hours after we'd been at the hotel."

"How do you know I hadn't unpacked and simply reclosed the bags?"

"When I went to hang up your coat, the closet was empty."

"This is all so silly," she said. "If you don't have anything more substantive to cover, I have other things to do."

"I do have a few additional questions," George said. "I'll try to make them brief. I assume you are the beneficiary of any insurance policies Wayne owned."

"Of course. He took his responsibilities seriously. Life insurance was an important part of his financial package, along with investments and savings."

"The airline?" George said. "Did he leave his share of SilverAir to you?"

The attorney spoke up. "Negotiations are currently underway regarding SilverAir's financial and management structure. I don't feel it is in Mrs. Silverton's best interests to discuss the matter at this time."

"I understand," George said. "Maybe we'll have a chance to talk some more on the flight to Boston. Thank you for your time."

George put his pen and pad away and stood.

I debated saying anything more, but decided it was necessary. "Just one other thing before we go," I said.

All eyes turned to me.

"I realize, Christine, that what you confided in me about Wayne's infidelities is a highly personal matter. But a murder has taken place. Don't you think you should share those thoughts with Inspector Sutherland? They could have a bearing on the case and—"

"I think that is very much out of place, Jessica," Christine said.

"I don't think this line of questioning is relevant," Bellnap said.

"It goes to motive," George said. "Mrs. Fletcher is right. If there are any factors that potentially impact this investigation, I urge you to be straightforward with me about them," he said to Christine.

Christine began to respond, but was interrupted by a knock at the door. She opened it to reveal her stepson, Jason, standing in the hall.

"Come in," she said pleasantly to him. "The inspector and Mrs. Fletcher are just leaving."

Chapter Fifteen

"Who's the young man?" George asked when the door closed behind us.

"That's right," I said. "You haven't had the pleasure. It's Jason Silverton, Wayne Silverton's son."

"Ah. Paying a visit to his stepmother?"

"Looks that way. What I find interesting is her greeting to him. As I told you, I was with Christine when he first showed up. She seemed horrified to see him, and he didn't have anything warm and affectionate to say to her, or about her. Her mood has obviously changed. I wonder why."

The elevator arrived and several people stepped back to make room for us. When we reached the ground floor, I asked, "Do you have time for us to talk a bit?"

"Afraid not, my dear. I have many things to do before we leave."

"Will you be riding with us to the airport?"

"No. I'll drive myself and use a car park at Stansted."

"All right. I'll see you on board then."

His eyes twinkled. "I'll see you at Stansted Airport in time for our departure. I know one thing."

"What's that?"

"Trying to solve a murder at thirty-five thousand feet will be a first for me."

"An ideal setup. All the suspects huddled together and nowhere to go."

"Let's hope so."

After George had left the hotel, I decided to go into the American Bar for tea, iced this time, and some quiet think time. I doubted the lounge would be crowded at that hour, but I was wrong. Still, I stayed, and was shown to a small table in a relatively peaceful corner. Peace was fleeting, however. I'd no sooner been served when Jed Richardson walked into the room.

"Mind company?" he asked.

"Not at all. Where's Barbara?"

"Out shopping, I'm afraid. I suspect we'll be traveling back to Boston a lot heavier than when we left."

He ordered a scotch, neat.

"I did some checking on our two pilots, Jess; even made a few phone calls to friends back in the States."

"I didn't mean for you to go to all that trouble, Jed."

"No trouble at all. They have interesting backgrounds."

"Tell me about it."

"Okay. First, there's Captain Caine. His flying record is pristine, no mishaps, no sanctions against him by the FAA or the airlines he's flown with."

"I sense a 'but' coming."

"Yeah, there is a 'but.' He was fired from the last airline he worked for because of his attitude."

"Attitude? About flying?"

"No, about authority. Seems he's got a short fuse, a really short fuse. It got him in trouble a couple of times, once with management, once with a passenger. He hit one."

"Hit a passenger?"

"That's right. Slugged this guy after they'd landed at LAX. This passenger, according to what Caine reported, mouthed off at him about the flight, said it was lousy, no food, that sort of thing. Nothing new about that these days. Planes are filled with disgruntled passengers. Plenty of air rage to go around. I know one thing. I'd hate to be a flight attendant in this atmosphere, standing at the open door to an aircraft and having to face hundreds of unhappy travelers. God, they come on dressed as though they were going to a mud wrestling competition, hauling steamer trunks that they try to shove into the overhead bins, surly from the minute they board. And who can blame them? They're treated like cattle, only cattle are better fed. That's why Wayne's notion to start an airline that treats passengers the way they used to be treated appeals to me. I tell you, Jessica, the worst thing that ever happened to air travel in the States was deregulation. It's created one hell of a mess."

I listened patiently to Jed's rant. I'd heard it many times before. I tended to agree with him, although I knew many people who would argue with his support of airline regulation.

I got him back on track. "Tell me more about Captain Caine's confrontation with this passenger."

"Right. This passenger evidently said some things to Caine that he didn't like and poked him in the chest to emphasize his point. Caine hauled off and punched the guy, which led to a civil suit against Caine and the airline. It was settled out of court, the terms sealed. But Caine lost his job over it."

"And ended up being hired by Wayne for Silver-Air," I said.

"Right. Like I say, he's a good pilot, fully qualified on the 767. Just don't say anything to set him off." He laughed. "With the number of qualified pilots having been laid off, I'm surprised that Wayne chose Caine, considering his temperament."

"I suppose anyone can lose his cool under the right circumstances," I said in Caine's defense.

"Not when you're wearing four stripes on your uniform sleeve and working for a major airline. Anyway, speaking of qualifications, the first officer, Carl Scherer, is an enigma."

"How so?"

"How he got to ride the right seat in an aircraft

like the 767. One minute he's flying small regional jets; the next thing you know he's 767-qualified."

"Are you saying that he's not certified to fly that aircraft?"

Jed shook his head and sipped his drink. "Oh, no, Jessica, he's FAA-certified all right. It's just that Wayne put him on the fast track to certification, plucked him from his job at the regional, paid for accelerated simulator and flight training in the 767, and got him certified in time for SilverAir going into service. Again, with lots of veteran 767 pilots laid off, you have to wonder why Wayne wanted Scherer so badly."

"We'll never get to ask him," I said.

"Afraid not. Well," Jed said, finishing his drink, "I'd better go check on Barbara, see if she's back yet and hasn't broken the bank. See you at seven."

It seemed that everyone I spoke to fueled the fires of speculation surrounding Wayne Silverton's murder. There was plenty of raw material to ponder. The problem was linking it up, finding correlations between this nugget of information and the next. Did the backgrounds of the cockpit crew, Captain Caine and First Officer Scherer, mean anything in the larger picture? As hard as I tried, I couldn't make the connection. I thought of the first officer's wife, Betsy Scherer, one of SilverAir's flight attendants who'd served us on the trip to London. I'd meant to ask Jed if it was unusual for an airline to hire a husband and wife, and particularly to have them work the same flight. My conclusion was that because Silver-Air was a small airline, it could do what the larger carriers wouldn't do, especially when a single individual like Wayne seemed to be calling all the shots.

Time to add to my written list in the hope that seeing things on paper would help clarify my thinking.

After packing my bag for the trip home, I did just that: sat at the desk in my suite and added to my notes. As I filled the pages, my mind filled even faster. I stared at what I'd written and thought of the wonderful writer, Kurt Vonnegut, who once said that he considered it somewhat silly to make a living putting little black marks on paper. While he was obviously being facetious, all those little black marks on my lined, yellow legal pad added up to nothing helpful.

I dropped my pen on the desk, sat back, exhaled a stream of frustration, and tried to will some sense into what I knew, and what I'd committed to writing. Wayne was murdered for one of two reasons (or possibly a combination of both):

Money.

Passion.

I'd eliminated most people in our entourage as suspects because they were not known to have a personal connection with Wayne, or a business/working relationship.

Christine Silverton (Victim's wife. Husband was a womanizer. Possible heiress to the airline.)

Churlson Vicks (British partner in airline. Unsavory reputation. Angry that victim brought in Casale as a partner.)

Salvatore Casale (Partner in airline, reputed to have mob connections. Henchmen in London at time of murder.)

Capt. Bill Caine (Known to have temper. Scornful of victim's position as airline's founder. Obvious romantic relationship with flight attendant Gina Molnari.)

Gina Molnari (Flight attendant. Caine's lover? Made snide remarks about Christine Silverton. Suicide attempt with Christine's sleeping pills. Could there have been a romantic link to victim?)

First Officer Carl Scherer (Victim put him on fast-track to fly 767. Why? Had easy access to Caine's knife.)

Betsy Scherer (Flight attendant married to Scherer. Possible link to victim? Learn more.)

John Slater (Male flight attendant. What was his relationship to Wayne? No reason to suspect him. More to learn.)

Jason Silverton (Latest entry on list. No love for victim, or stepmother, Christine. Claims he now owns part of airline. Criminal record. Was he at the airport that night?)

I'd obviously discounted an act of random violence, committed by someone totally unrelated to the victim. There was no evidence of robbery. Had Wayne insulted someone at Stansted Airport, so much so that it prompted the man or woman to kill? Unlikely. Besides, how would someone like that find and use Captain Caine's knife?

No, it had to be one of the people on my list of primary suspects.

Which one?

I called George.

"Sorry to bother you," I said, "but I have a question. Has anything new developed with those two men detained at Heathrow, the ones allegedly associated with Mr. Casale?"

"Your timing is good, Jessica. I just received a synopsis of their interrogation. They admit to having been at Stansted Airport the night of the murder, but claim they went there to catch a flight to Paris. My people checked out their story and it has, at least, some credence. There was a flight leaving for Paris that they tried to get on. It was full, and they were on a standby basis. As it turned out, they never made that flight and went directly to Heathrow to try their chances there."

"But they *were* at Stansted."

"Yes. The question is: How would they have gotten hold of the captain's knife?"

"Mr. Casale. He had access to Caine's bag. He could have given it to these men with the intention of framing the captain."

"Perhaps."

"It doesn't hold up well, does it?" I said. "I'm

grasping at straws. The usual modus operandi of men like them would have involved a gun, wouldn't it?"

"Without a doubt, but getting a gun through airport security is a little more difficult these days, at least that's the general idea," he said, chuckling.

"How are your preparations for leaving coming?"

"Fine, just fine, although I'm afraid I've made some of my mates here jealous, getting a free transatlantic flight to the States on a spanking new airline. I'll have to bring back gifts."

"Hopefully including the murderer all nicely packaged with a big bow."

"I like that visual, Jessica. My superiors aren't especially happy about the plane being allowed to leave. They've suggested it be impounded until the murderer is identified and taken into custody."

"But they relented."

"It was pointed out to them that we can't very well detain more than a hundred American citizens, many of them from the press and local governments, without more justification. Seems a judge substantiated that position when the higher-ups petitioned the court to delay the departure."

"Sounds like a wise decision."

"I think so. Don't hesitate to call. See you in a bit."

I checked my watch. I'd agreed to meet my Cabot Cove traveling companions in the main dining room for dinner at five thirty, and it was almost that now.

I picked up my handbag, opened the door, and gasped. Standing before me was Churlson Vicks, his fist poised to knock.

"You startled me, Mr. Vicks. I was just leaving and—"

"I know this is an unwanted intrusion, Mrs. Fletcher," he said pressing me back into the room, "and I apologize profusely for it. But I must have a word with you. I promise not to take up too much of your time."

"I'm meeting people for dinner, Mr. Vicks."

"I'll get right to the point," he said. "You're aware, of course, of the sudden and distinctly unwelcome emergence of the young Mr. Silverton."

"Yes, I am."

"I believe I indicated to you earlier that it is not in his best interests to make his outrageous—ludicrous, actually—claim that he owns a stake in SilverAir based upon an ancient letter from his father."

I nodded, remembering the brief exchange we'd had.

"I come to you because, quite frankly, you seem to be the only one in this group with any common sense."

"I don't know why you would say that, Mr. Vicks. You don't know me. But go on."

"You must dissuade Christine and this young punk from pushing forward their claim that SilverAir is now in their control."

"Just a second," I said, holding up a hand for emphasis. "First of all, you say it's *their* claim. I hardly think Christine and Jason would work in concert."

"Mrs. Fletcher, when the ownership of an airline is at stake, stranger bedfellows than those two have gotten together beneath the sheets." He came forward, his voice becoming more urgent, although I wasn't sure it was genuine. "I reiterate, Mrs. Fletcher, that Salvatore is not a man who takes such things lightly."

"You're saying that the lives of Christine and her stepson are in danger?"

"It's a distinct possibility. I am not threatening that, you understand, but there are others whose actions I do not control."

"And what is it you want from me?"

"Talk to Christine, Mrs. Fletcher. She'll listen to you. Make her realize that she is courting terrible trouble if she continues this unreasonable quest to take over the airline. Show her that this stepson of hers is a low-life hustler, a con man of the first order. I had my people check his police record. He's been arrested a dozen times."

"Six, I believe."

He looked momentarily surprised. "Yes, perhaps I exaggerate. But six or twelve, he's a common criminal. No good can come from her tossing in with him. Don't you see?"

"I must admit, Mr. Vicks, that I'm having a problem at this moment giving what you claim a great deal of credibility. Are you sure you aren't asking me to intercede in some way with Christine to benefit you and Mr. Casale financially, to get her to back off on her pursuit of her husband's ownership share in the airline?"

How could you possibly think that of me? his expression said.

I walked to the door and opened it. "I really must go, Mr. Vicks. I'm afraid I can't be of any help in this matter. My major concern is not who owns SilverAir. It's who murdered Wayne Silverton."

He nodded, walked into the hall, turned and said, "Don't say I didn't warn you, Mrs. Fletcher. If something should happen to Christine, it will be on your conscience. As for her stepson, no one's conscience should be bothered if he meets a tragic end. Good evening."

Chapter Sixteen

Vicks's ominous warning lingered in the air after the door was closed.

Was there any substance to his claim that the lives of Christine and Jason Silverton were in danger from Salvatore Casale? I doubted it. It was evident from what the Englishman had said that he and Casale, fighting for control of SilverAir, were looking for allies. Why me? I had no vested interest in the disposition of the airline, nor did I have influence over Christine. As for Jason, whether or not he ended up owning a piece of the company started by his father was of no concern to me. That would be resolved through appropriate legal channels.

But I wasn't about to summarily dismiss Vicks's warning of possible physical harm coming to them. If there was any validity to Casale's reputation as a mafioso—and if he'd had a hand in Wayne's murder—it was possible that he wouldn't hesitate to use strong-arm tactics to get his way in a potentially lucrative business deal, which SilverAir obviously represented.

My concerns were primarily about Christine. Her behavior since Wayne's death had been off-putting, but that didn't lessen my compassion for her. That she was under a lot of pressure went without saying. I just hoped that the impact of losing her husband hadn't clouded her judgment when it came to pursuing her legal rights to the airline.

Jason was another matter. I'd found his brash manner and arrogant disregard for the fact that his father had been murdered to be distasteful, at best. But I also realized that although he was not a simpatico young man, his childhood—at least the little I'd learned about it—had not been what you'd call nurturing and loving. I wasn't making excuses for him. Millions of kids emerge from less than ideal childhoods and go on to become responsible, sensitive, caring adults. But if Vicks was right—and I had to give his claims some weight—Jason's life could be in danger, along with that of his stepmother.

I didn't have time to chew on it for very long because I was due downstairs for dinner and was already late (so much for my reputation of always being on time). I joined my friends in the River Restaurant, a large, magnificent dining room decorated in soft salmon and peach colors, with large windows affording a view of the Thames through the trees. I'd enjoyed many meals in that lovely setting, going back to when Frank and I had honeymooned at the Savoy.

On one trip to London after Frank had died, I was there over the Thanksgiving holiday. The British, of course, don't celebrate our Thanksgiving, and I found myself yearning for a touch of that most traditional of American holidays. The concierge at the hotel in which I was staying suggested the River Restaurant at the Savoy. "They serve your traditional Thanksgiving menu, I believe, madam," he said. He was right. The restaurant was filled with like-minded Americans enjoying turkey carved at tableside and all the trimmings. It was a dinner I've never forgotten, a hundred American strangers gathered together like one big family.

"All set to go home, Mrs. F.?" Mort asked, as he held a chair out for me.

"I think so."

We were eight at the table: the Richardsons, the Metzgers, the Shevlins, Seth and I. They'd ordered smoked salmon, thinly sliced by a white-coated gentleman who looked as though he'd been doing it for decades, and I decided to join them.

Jed's wife, Barbara, was dressed in a fashionable outfit, a lime green linen pantsuit, which I commented on.

"I found this amazing seamstress," she said, glowing, "who made this for me in a couple of hours."

Jed laughed. "I'd better alert the cockpit crew that

we might have a weight-and-balance problem for the flight back."

"I didn't buy *that* much, Jed," Barbara said, poking his arm.

Seth reported on his visit with his newfound physician friend. "They've got problems with their medical delivery system," he said, "but so do we back home. Frankly, I don't see why a country like ours can't come up with a way for everyone to be covered."

That sparked a debate between Seth and Jim about the pros and cons of universal health care, which the rest of us stayed out of. It was Susan who finally introduced the topic of the Silverton murder.

"I have this eerie feeling," she said, "about flying home with a murderer."

"Amen," Maureen said. "Jessica, has George Sutherland made any headway in solving it?"

"These things take time," I said. "It's only been a couple of days. You know he'll be traveling with us on the return flight."

"Not especially comforting," Seth grumbled.

"He's not there to comfort us," I said. "He's going to use the flight as another opportunity to question people."

"And what if he ends up identifying the murderer?" Seth asked. "Whoever did it is likely to raise a fuss, wouldn't you say? Maybe put everyone on the plane in jeopardy."

"I'm sure George wouldn't allow that to happen," I said.

Maureen gave me a knowing look. "And what about the other case he's working on?" she asked.

"What other case?" Susan asked.

"The budding romance between Jessica and George."

Seth turned to me. "Is that true, Jessica?" he asked. "Is there something I should know about?"

"If there were," I said, "you'd be the first to know."

"Hey, wait a minute," Jim said. "I'm the mayor of Cabot Cove. I should be the first to know."

They bantered back and forth about that subject until it was time to order our dinners. Had we been eating later, we would have enjoyed a dance band that performs each evening, a throwback to another era when such orchestras were standard fare in posh restaurants.

It was a shame that we had to rush through our meal. The ambiance of the River Restaurant is such that you want to linger forever. But we eventually ran out of time, left the table, went to our rooms to collect our luggage, and joined up again in front of the Savoy where a fleet of limousines waited to whisk us to Stansted Airport. The weather was still dreadful. The sky seemed to have ruptured, allowing rain to cascade down like a waterfall. In addition, a wind had kicked up, sending the rain horizontally and rendering the large umbrellas wielded by the limo drivers virtually useless. But they did their best to get us to their vehicles as dry as possible, and eventually everyone was settled in, happy to be out of the deluge. I had no idea how everyone was grouped in the other limousines. All I knew was that those of us from Cabot Cove were together, and I was happy about that.

It was a slow, tedious trip, but eventually the airport's lights came into view and we pulled up as close as possible to the entrance. Again, with an assortment of black umbrellas providing some protection from the elements, we were escorted inside the terminal and asked to wait until further notice in an area roped off for us.

I saw Christine enter, accompanied by her attorney, Mr. Bellnap, and her stepson, Jason. *Is he going with us on the flight?* I wondered. They stood together, apart from the main group. Following them was a bevy of press who'd been on the flight to London, and some of the politicians from back home who'd also been invited. A few minutes later, Churlson Vicks and Salvatore Casale made their appearance. They ignored our staging area and walked by, heads down, men with weighty issues on their minds.

"Where's the crew?" Mort asked. "Can't go without *them*."

"I'm sure they came to the airport earlier," I offered. "There's always a lot of preflight business to take care of."

"I hope their first piece of business is this weather," Seth said. "They'd have to be nuts to take off in this storm."

"They won't do anything that isn't safe," I said, hoping my words would ease his worries. I didn't admit that I, too, was apprehensive about flying in such severe weather. Repeated slashes of lightning could be seen through huge floor-to-ceiling windows, and deafening thunder made sure that no one forgot Mother Nature's power.

I'd become acutely aware of weather and its potential to damage planes, even the largest and most sophisticated of them, when taking flying lessons from Jed in Cabot Cove. As he often told me, many private plane fatalities could have been avoided if the pilots had respected the weather. Accidents labeled weather-related, he'd said, were most often caused by pilots ignoring weather conditions in which it was dangerous to fly. "Doctors," he said, "are the worst culprits. They think they're God and have to get back home for surgery that's scheduled the next day. They take off regardless of the weather, and some never make it."

The weather was causing a lot of apprehension in our group. One woman, a Boston city council member, stated that she wasn't about to get on a plane in those conditions. A writer for an aviation business journal echoed her protestations. And Seth was, I judged, ready to join them. But before a mutiny fully developed, the flight attendant, Betsy Scherer, arrived and announced that we were ready to board.

We followed her through the terminal to SilverAir's gate. The building was teeming with people; a number of outgoing flights had been canceled, according to the digital departure-and-arrival boards we passed, and incoming flights were seriously delayed, creating a domino effect. No planes arriving meant no planes available to depart.

I'd been looking for George ever since we entered the terminal. Surely, he wouldn't miss the flight unless the weather had seriously delayed his drive to the airport. I considered not boarding and waiting for him in the departure lounge, but decided that it wouldn't accomplish anything. I stood in line as a uniformed SilverAir ground employee checked off passengers from a clipboard as they reached the entrance to the Jetway.

"Fletcher," I said when I reached him. "Jessica Fletcher."

He made a mark next to my name and waved me through. I lingered just inside the Jetway for the rest of the Cabot Cove group to catch up. We walked together toward the open door to the 767 where Gina Molnari and First Officer Carl Scherer stood greeting passengers. A large, clear Plexiglas insert in the side of the Jetway gave me a view of a portion of the cockpit. Captain Bill Caine was in the customary captain's left-hand seat, his hands going to various knobs and buttons as he ran through his preflight rituals.

"Good evening, Mrs. Fletcher," Gina said.

"Good evening," I replied. "Glad to see you're looking so well."

"Feeling fine," she said. Her tight expression said she wasn't at all happy to see me.

I stepped inside the aircraft and looked to my left through the open cockpit door. Caine turned and saw me, nodded, and went back to his chores. I chose a seat and looked in vain for George. Christine and Jason Silverton boarded. The icy look on Christine's face when she saw me was evident even from where I sat. Jason was all smiles as he chatted with Betsy Scherer.

Where is George?

A clap of thunder seemed to shake the plane as it sat at the gate. I glanced at Seth, who'd already buckled himself into his seat, and whose expression was one of abject fear. Seth is a man who seems never to be intimidated by anything—except flying. I've been on many flights where his grip on the armrests was enough to dent them, and his knuckles were as white as freshly fallen snow. But it was obvious that his anxiety level on this evening was especially high.

I leaned over him and suggested, "Why don't you try self-hypnosis? It worked for me when I couldn't sleep."

"*Ayuh,*" he said. "I may do that."

"Pretend you're flying the plane," I said, remembering what Jed had told me. When he was a captain with a major airline, he'd taken part in a company-sponsored series of seminars for people whose fear of flying was acute, and whose lives were negatively impacted by their fears. "People are afraid to fly," he'd said, "because they lack control. We teach 'em to take an active part in the flying process, even rise up a little from their seats on takeoff to make the plane lighter."

"I'll be all right," Seth said, not sounding as though he meant it. "Hypnosis won't make this ugly weather any better."

I patted his hand and walked toward the rear of the plane. I'd learned years ago that when Seth is dealing with a problem, it's usually best to leave him alone. I could have cited statistics to him: Your chances of being involved in an aircraft accident are about one in eleven million; chances of being killed in an auto accident are one in five thousand. Driving to the airport poses a far greater risk than getting on a plane, as evidenced by more than fifty thousand people killed in auto accidents each year. But none of that would have helped Seth at that moment. Unless the rain and wind suddenly stopped, and a rainbow appeared, there was little anyone could say, or do, to alleviate his concerns.

I'd stopped to chat with one of the reporters when Jason Silverton approached from where he and Christine had taken seats at the front of the passenger cabin.

"Hello, Mrs. Fletcher," he said.

"Hello, Jason."

He said through a toothy grin, "You look surprised that I'm on the flight."

"Not at all. It appears you've made up with your stepmother."

He glanced back at Christine. "Yeah. I'm irresistible." He smiled at me, but it wasn't a pleasant smile. "Makes sense for me to be on this flight," he said. "A shame Dad couldn't make it. Of course, he wouldn't be occupying a seat. He'd be down below in the cargo hold. But the police wouldn't release his body. So he stays back in jolly old England."

How sad for Wayne, I thought, that his only child had nothing but callous comments to make about his father.

"Now that I own a piece of this airline," Jason said, "I'll be on lots of SilverAir flights."

"Has the ownership question been settled?" I asked.

"Not yet, but it will be." He looked past me to where Vicks and Casale sat huddled in adjacent seats poring over a sheaf of papers. "Those two clowns think they can bully me out of the picture, but I don't scare easy. Between Christine and me, we'll show them who's really the boss."

"If you say so, Jason," I said, eager to escape his gloating. "I wish you well."

"Maybe you'd like to write a book about me," he said. "I'll bet I'm the youngest airline owner in the world."

"That may be," I said. "Excuse me."

I joined Jed and Barbara Richardson where they'd

just accepted coffee from the young male flight attendant, John Slater.

"Think we'll go?" I asked Jed.

"It's a toss-up," he said. "Depends on what the captain up front decides. It's his call."

"What would you do?" I asked.

He smiled and sipped. "Me? I always went with the most conservative approach, Jess. But I don't want to second-guess Captain Caine. It's his ship, like the captain of an ocean liner. The only difference is he can't conduct marriages."

"Speaking of that," Barbara said, winking at me and pointing to the front of the aircraft where George Sutherland had just come aboard.

I gave Barbara my best disapproving look and headed up the aisle. George looked frazzled. His tan trench coat was rain-darkened, and his hair was wet, too. He carried a small, leather overnight bag along with a well-worn leather briefcase with a shoulder strap.

"I was getting worried," I said. "I was afraid you wouldn't make it."

"I had my doubts, too," he said. "Last-minute snafus at the office, and slow going on the roads. But here I am. Anything new?"

"Always something new, it seems, but I'll fill you in later."

First Officer Scherer passed us, entered the cockpit, and closed the door behind him.

"Any talk of scuttling the flight?" George asked.

"No. As far as I know, we're going."

Mort joined us. "Evening, Inspector," he said.

"Good evening to you, Sheriff."

"Any progress?" Mort asked.

"Bits and pieces, that's all," George said.

Mort leaned close to George's ear and whispered just loud enough for me to hear, too, "I've got my weapon with me in case there's trouble."

"That's good to hear," George said. "I'm glad you're with us."

Until Mort mentioned carrying his revolver with him, I hadn't given a thought to weapons aboard. I knew that Mort was allowed to carry his weapon whenever he flew because of his status as a law enforcement officer, and it was likely that Captain Caine and First Officer Scherer carried guns, too, under the new FAA regulations allowing, even encouraging, cockpit crews to be armed. But what about other passengers? Because we were a nonscheduled flight, security had been handled by SilverAir ground personnel, not government-sanctioned and trained officers.

I looked around the cabin. Anyone could be carrying a weapon of some sort, a realization that didn't sit well with me.

I accepted a club soda from Gina Molnari. George asked for a Coke.

"Excuse me, Inspector," Churlson Vicks said.

"Yes?"

"I'd like a word with you."

"I'm listening," said George.

"I'll be blunt, sir. I don't like the fact that you're joining us for the purpose of trying to identify a killer."

"That's my job, Mr. Vicks."

"This is a public relations flight. We've got a lot of press aboard. Don't want them distracted from the business at hand."

"Murder is always the business at hand," George said. "We believe someone on this plane murdered Mr. Silverton. With everyone leaving London to return home to the States, the chances of bringing the killer to justice are slim, if not nonexistent. I really don't have any choice but to pursue it while the guilty party is still in our midst."

"Well," Vicks huffed, "that may be how you see it, Inspector, but I intend to have a word with your superiors the moment I return to London."

"By all means, sir. Please do."

I had the feeling that such threats had been made to George before, and that he wasn't unduly concerned about any of them.

Captain Caine's voice came over the PA system.

"Ladies and gentlemen, this is your captain from the flight deck. We're getting close to push-back, and we'll be on our way shortly. I'd like to ask you to find your seats, settle down, and buckle up in anticipation of our departure. Cabin crew, please cross-check."

I'd sat next to Seth on the flight to London and

assumed I'd do it again. But Jim had taken my seat and was engaged in an animated conversation with Seth, freeing me to sit with George in the row behind.

"I had a conversation with Jed Richardson this afternoon," I reported, "about the backgrounds of Captain Caine and the first officer, Carl Scherer."

"Anything of particular interest in what he told you?"

I repeated what Jed had said, that Caine had been fired from a previous job for attitudinal problems and for having struck a passenger, and that Wayne Silverton had taken special pains to accelerate Scherer's rise from a regional pilot of smaller aircraft to 767 certification.

"Why would he do that?" George mused aloud. "There must be plenty of pilots out there looking for work who are certified to fly this aircraft."

"I don't have an answer," I said, "and I've been searching my brain for one ever since hearing it."

Our conversation was interrupted by Gina Molnari's voice over the PA, informing us that our seat belts were to be secured, loose items stored beneath the seat in front of us or in the overhead bins, meal trays securely fastened, and our seats in a full upright position. A video on aircraft safety played on the screens through the passenger cabin.

"Seems we're on our way," George muttered.

As he said it, the brightest flash of lightning and most deafening roar of thunder all evening sent a garish streak of light, like a photographer's strobe, throughout the cabin, and the thunder elicited expressions of dismay throughout the cabin.

"*Gorry!*" Seth said in a loud voice.

"Yes," I thought as the plane was pushed back from the gate, the rain coming in pulsating splashes against the small window. "Gorry, indeed!"

Chapter Seventeen

The wind buffeted the plane as we taxied to the runway, lightning and thunder accompanying us every inch of the way.

"There's only one plane ahead of us for takeoff," Caine announced over the PA.

That represented good news to everyone aboard, not because it meant we would be taking off soon, but because it said that there was another pilot willing to fly in this weather. I knew, of course, that once we reached our assigned cruising altitude, we'd be above the foul weather and enjoying relatively smooth skies. But until then, I grasped George's forearm, and he placed a hand over mine. I remembered that Captain Caine had invited me up front again for the takeoff but had obviously forgotten, or decided the flight deck wasn't the place for an amateur that night. Whatever the reason, it was fine with me.

Our turn came. The 767's twin jet engines roared to life, and we began our takeoff roll, slowly at first until the engines' thrust overcame inertia, then picking up speed and eating up runway, faster and faster. The increased speed sent more air over and under the wings, creating "lift" due to their unique shape—relatively flat on the underside, slightly curved on top—the Bernoulli Principle that allows planes to fly at work. The wheels bounced less as gravity's grip on them decreased, and we were airborne, blasting through the rain and wind and heavy cloud cover in search of better conditions.

"*Gorry!*" I heard Seth exclaim again, louder this time.

We continued to climb for another ten or fifteen minutes. Eventually, we broke free of the clouds and were in calm, pitch black air, the wings' flashing lights and the stars the only outside illumination. There were audible sighs of relief. The Boston councilwoman had cried during the takeoff roll but was now relatively calm. The flight attendants left their seats and started serving drinks again, and hot and cold hors d'oeuvres. A menu in the seat-back pockets promised a three-course dinner, but those of us who'd already eaten had no enthusiasm for another meal.

"Well," George said after it was announced that we were free to move about the cabin but should keep our seat belts loosely fastened when seated, "I'd best get started."

"Do you want to make an announcement that you'll be interviewing people?" I asked.

"I think not," he said. "Everyone knows why I'm here. I would like you to tag along, however."

"Of course I will," I said, not adding that I would have been disappointed if I hadn't been asked.

He stood and surveyed the cabin. "See that area where four seats are grouped together around that table?" he asked.

"Yes. Perfect for a business conference. And a murder interrogation."

"We'll set up shop there."

We joined others who'd gotten out of their seats and were milling about, drinks in hand, chatting about myriad things. Churlson Vicks had gone to the lavatory, leaving Sal Casale sitting alone.

"Good evening, Mr. Casale," George said.

"Oh, you're the inspector," Calsale said.

"I wonder if you'd join me and Mrs. Fletcher over there."

Casale looked to where George pointed. "Sure, why not?"

We took three of the four seats. George laid a pad of paper and a pen on the table, crossed his legs, sat back, and smiled. "You obviously know why I wish to speak with you, Mr. Casale."

"I'd be a moron if I didn't," said Casale. "You want to know if I killed Wayne. Not a chance. Wayne and I were in business for many years, first in Vegas real estate, then in this stupid airline deal. You know why I say it's a stupid deal? I'll tell you why. You know any airline that's making money? They're all belly-up. Even when they make money, it's chump change. Yeah, some of those low-fare airlines are doing okay, but Wayne wanted to go high-end. I went along because there was something—I don't know, something fancy about it, you know, like the jet set." He, too, sat back and shook his head. "Did I kill him? Hell, no. But I think I know who did."

"I'd be interested in hearing your theory, Mr. Casale," George said.

"Him." He pointed at Jason Silverton, who stood talking with Mort Metzger.

"Please explain," George said.

"He's a punk. Wayne used to talk about him to me. The kid turned out to be a foul ball after all his old man did for him. The kid takes a walk and disappears for years, but shows up when Wayne is dead, carrying a letter he claims Wayne wrote to him years ago." He guffawed. "Can you believe it? I sure don't."

"What does the letter say?" I asked.

"I'd show it to you, only I don't have it with me. Vicks gave it to his lawyer. Barristers, he calls them. Doesn't matter what you call them. Thieves. They're all thieves."

"The letter gives Jason his father's share in Silver-Air?" I said.

"Ain't that a joke? What does the kid do? He takes that phony letter and shows it to Christine, the wicked stepmother. She can't stand the sight of the kid, but hustler that she is, she sees how they can gang up and claim the airline for themselves. Nice people, huh?"

George ignored Casale's condemnation of Christine and Jason and asked about the two men who were detained at Heathrow, men with reputed ties to Casale's criminal activities.

"I'll own that newspaper," Casale said. "It'll be in my pocket before they know it."

"The men are alleged to work for you," I said.

"Right. They do. They're business associates."

"From what I understand of their resumes," George said, "they hardly qualify as businessmen in the traditional sense."

"Maybe not traditional the way you define it, Inspector. Different strokes."

"I understand," George continued, "that Mr. Silverton didn't always live up to the promises he made to his business partners."

The surprised look on Casale's swarthy face seemed genuine. "You can't prove that by me," he said. "Sure, Wayne could cut a tough deal, and if somebody tried to screw him, he knew how to take it out on them. But me? I never had any trouble with him. You think I would've stayed in business with him this long if he'd tried to ace me out of what's due me? Forget about it." He waved his hand for emphasis. "Satisfied?" he asked.

"For the moment," George said.

Casale noticed that Vicks was watching and waved him over. "Hey, Churlson—that's some name, huh?—the inspector here wants to ask you some questions."

I had to smile at Casale's flamboyant style. He was like an actor out of Central Casting for a television show such as *The Sopranos*, or a movie like *The Godfather* or *Goodfellas*. I believed him when he said he didn't have a beef with Wayne and hadn't been behind his murder. But that represented only my snap judgment.

Vicks took the seat vacated by Casale.

George started by asking the Englishman the same thing he'd asked Casale, whether Wayne Silverton had been aboveboard and honest with him in their business dealings.

"If I say that he wasn't," Vicks responded, "it would give me a motive to kill the man, wouldn't it?"

"Perhaps," George replied.

"Well," said Vicks, "I didn't consider Wayne to be an especially honest man. He made promises that he didn't keep, but that didn't make him unusual. Not in the business world. It's survival of the fittest, dog-eat-dog, war!" He said to me, "You've seen plenty of it in your own country, Mrs. Fletcher, your top executives going on trial. Oh, yes, everyone is out to get what he can, and all the ethics taught in those bloody business schools can be tossed in the trash. Wayne was as ruthless as the next businessman, but he wasn't the best at it. Oh, no. He met his match with me."

"Does that include killing him?" I asked, surprised that I'd asked such a blunt question. A small smile formed on George's lips.

"No."

"Did you go directly into London from Stansted after you landed?" George asked.

"Of course I did."

"In one of the limos?"

"In my own limousine," Vicks said. "My driver met me."

"I'm sure he'll verify that," George said.

"He'd damn well better or he can find himself another job."

I said, "Mr. Vicks, you told me that your partner, Mr. Casale, was capable of hurting Jason Silverton if he continued to pursue his claim to his father's share of SilverAir."

Vicks lowered his voice. "I wouldn't want him to know that I said that."

I continued. "Mr. Casale thinks Jason Silverton might be the one who murdered his father. Do you agree with that?"

"Why, yes, I do. Didn't I already tell you that, Mrs. Fletcher?"

"We have a long plane ride, Mr. Vicks," George said. "Perhaps you'll think of something else before we land that will be helpful to me."

"Seems obvious on the surface," Vicks said. "That young hooligan killed his father to gain control of the airline."

"Using a bogus letter?"

"Yes, that's exactly how I see it. Are you quite finished with me?"

"For now," George said. "Thank you for your time."

When Vicks was gone, George said, "I'd love a single-malt scotch, but that would constitute drinking while on duty, wouldn't it?"

"I'm afraid so," I said, "although this is very special duty."

"Still—"

"Whom are you going to talk to next?" I asked.

"The young man, Jason. We have no indication that he was at the airport the night of the murder, do we?"

"Not that I know of. I'll get him for you. First I want to check on Seth. He was terribly uneasy about flying in that dreadful weather."

I'd become aware while sitting with George that there was intense interest in what we were doing in our little corner of the cabin. Some people had pretended to simply pass by and pause with their ears cocked. Others seemed to be trying to read lips. I was sure I'd be stopped at some point and asked about what had transpired, and reminded myself that it would be wrong to divulge anything.

Mort was the first to strike.

"How's it going, Mrs. F.?" he asked.

"Fine, Mort."

"That British guy, Vicks, looked nervous when he left you. What did he have to say?"

"Nothing of use," I said. "How's Seth?"

"See for yourself."

My dear friend had fallen asleep in his seat, his head resting on a pillow wedged against his window, a silver blanket with the airline's logo on it covering him. I smiled. Extreme tension can leave a person exhausted, and I was glad he'd given into it. The incessant whine of the jet engines, and the movement of the plane through the air, with an occasional bump, probably also contributed to his sleepiness. It was having its effect on me, too.

"Excuse me," I said to Jason. "Inspector Sutherland would like to speak with you."

"Grill me, you mean," he said. "I'd rather talk to the sheriff here. He's a real cop, not like those clowns at Scotland Yard."

He walked in George's direction.

"He's got some attitude," Mort said.

"Very unpleasant."

"I've been putting things together, Mrs. F."

"That's right. You said you had a theory about the murder."

"Not really a theory. I've picked up pieces here and there, news reports, gossip, slips of the tongue. And no thanks to you." He laughed and patted my shoulder. "Just kidding."

"I admit I haven't said much, Mort. I've tried to be discreet."

"And that's the right thing to do. Anyway, I've heard about how our captain's knife was used to kill Wayne and that his prints were on it."

"I'd say you've done more than just pick up bits and pieces, Mort."

"I've done okay. At any rate, Mrs. F., the logical suspect is Captain Caine. Am I right?"

"Yes, you are right. But let's not rush to judgment."

"I agree with that. Let's say Caine didn't do it. That means somebody stole his knife and used it to kill Wayne, maybe hoping to frame the captain."

"Right again. George and I have discussed that possibility."

"So—"

I waited.

"So, Mrs. F., if I were the investigating officer on the case, I'd start with whoever had the easiest access to that knife."

I nodded.

"Put that person on the top of your suspect list—after Caine, of course—and work down to the one who would have had the toughest job getting to the knife."

"A good idea, Mort. I'll mention it to George."

"No, Mrs. F., I'll do it. He might take it better coming from a fellow law enforcement officer."

"I think you're right," I said. "Why don't you spend some time with him after he's finished with Jason."

"I'll do that." He sighed. "Nice and smooth now, huh?"

"Always nice to get up above the weather."

I gravitated to the front of the plane where Christine sat alone reading a sheaf of legal-looking papers, half-glasses perched on the end of her nose.

"Hi," I said.

She looked over her glasses and smiled. "Hello, Jessica. Sit." She patted the empty chair next to her.

"You look busy," I said.

"My eyes are giving out reading all these legal documents. I'd enjoy the break."

I'd no sooner settled into the large, comfortable leather chair when she said, "I think I owe you an apology."

"For what?"

"For the way I've been acting."

"Christine," I said, "you were entitled to act any way you had to. You've lost your husband in a brutal way, and you're up to your neck in the business fallout from it. No apologies necessary."

"You're as understanding as your reputation says. You're very much beloved back in Cabot Cove."

"That's always nice to hear."

"I wish I'd gotten to know you better. Those trips to Wayne's hometown were much too brief—and busy."

"I know. There never seems to be enough time to spend with people we enjoy." I indicated the papers on her lap. "Business?"

"Yes. My lawyer—you met him—brought enough papers to fill a couple of file cabinets." She snickered. "Computers were supposed to result in a paperless society. It seems they create more paper than ever before."

"I've noticed that, too."

"I see that your friend from Scotland Yard is questioning people in the rear of the plane."

"An unusual venue to interview people about a murder," I said.

"I suppose that although he's already spoken with me, he'll want to do it again."

"Probably. Mind a few questions from me?"

"Why did I sense that you'd be asking questions, Jessica? You're not only loved in Cabot Cove, you have a reputation as an inveterate snoop." She grabbed my arm. "And I don't mean that in a pejorative sense. You're a very curious lady."

"A curse of my profession," I said. "No offense." I made sure that no one was within hearing distance when I said, "Christine, you told me that Wayne was quite a ladies' man. I know this is a painful topic, but—"

"It was more painful when he was alive, Jessica, than it is now. Ask whatever you wish about it."

"Are any of the women with whom he was involved on this flight?"

Her smile was rueful. "In other words," she said, "was one of them his murderer?"

I confirmed with a nod.

"I assume you're referring to Gina and Betsy."

"That's right. I'm not accusing them, Christine. I'm just trying to fit the pieces into the puzzle. Of course,

I can ask them directly—and will. But any information from you would make it easier."

She rested her head against the seat back and closed her eyes. When she opened them, she turned to face me. "They both had their fling with Wayne."

"Both?" I didn't expect that would be her answer.

"Uh huh. Wayne played his own version of the Hollywood casting couch, Jessica. Some men use expensive gifts to keep their mistresses interested in them. Wayne did that, too, of course. With all his business acumen, he wasn't very adept at concealing those purchases. A credit card receipt would show up now and then for a piece of jewelry, expensive handbag, or hotel stay that had nothing to do with me."

Her admission of her deceased husband's multiple infidelities was painful to listen to, and I considered getting off that subject. But what she was saying might have bearing on the murder, and I wanted to develop as much information as possible.

"Ms. Molnari and Mrs. Scherer received such gifts?" I asked.

She shrugged. "I don't know. Probably. In their cases, Wayne used the appeal of working for a fancy new upscale airline as the lure. He insisted upon personally interviewing and selecting SilverAir's flight attendants. I told him that because I had once been a stewardess, I should assume that role. But he was adamant, and I knew why. I think Wayne truly believed that I didn't know about the other women.

Besides being a dreamer, he could be terribly naïve about some things."

She straightened in her chair and laughed. "Do you remember that scandal at TWA years ago when the airline introduced a program to encourage the wives of businessmen to travel with their husbands?"

"No, I don't."

"It caused quite a stir, Jessica. Someone in TWA's PR department came up with the plan, and it was initially very successful. Wives received a discount when accompanying their husbands on business trips."

"Sounds like a good idea."

"Oh, it was. But then some bright guy in public relations decided to take it a step further. The airline sent a letter of thanks to every wife who had supposedly flown with her husband on business trips. Of course, many such 'wives' weren't wives at all. They were secretaries or girlfriends, and you can imagine how many divorces resulted from that letter arriving in the mail."

"A perfect example of taking a good idea too far," I said.

"There are lots of stories like that in the airline business, Jessica. That's why I love it so. Sorry. I know I interrupted your train of thought. Gina and Betsy were handpicked by Wayne. They're union, of course, and receive union wages. But in going through the books, I saw that Wayne was paying them cash bonuses off the books. When Bill Caine found out about it, he was furious."

"Oh? Why would he be upset that Wayne was doing that?"

"Isn't it obvious? Bill and Gina have been having an affair since they started working for SilverAir. Bill came to me and said that if Wayne as much as laid a hand on Gina again, he'd kill him."

"He said that? He would 'kill him'?"

"His words precisely."

"Did you tell Wayne what Caine had said?"

"Yes."

"And?"

"He laughed it off, denied that he and Gina had been sexually involved. Of course, I knew differently."

"Did Caine ever confront Wayne about it directly?"

"I don't think so. Bill Caine is lucky to have this job. His reputation in the industry isn't what you'd call pristine."

"So I understand."

"But there was no love lost between them. Frankly, I'd been rooting for Bill to punch Wayne in the nose. Maybe that would have woken him up. Too late now, though. Does that sound terrible?"

"Not at all. Sometimes people need a good punch in the nose to wake them up to appreciate what they already have. Why didn't you tell Inspector Sutherland what Caine said to Wayne?"

"I'd forgotten about it until now."

Not something easily forgotten, I thought.

"What about Betsy?" I asked. "She's married to the first officer."

Christine's roll of her eyes said much.

"That bad?" I said.

She looked to where Betsy was serving dinner to a couple of male passengers who obviously hadn't eaten before the flight.

"Isn't she cute?" Christine said derisively. "Miss all-American-girl cheerleader. The older Wayne got, the younger the women he pursued. She may look like all peaches and cream, Jessica, but she's hard as steel."

It was hard to reconcile Betsy Scherer's exterior personality with Christine's assessment of her, but I accepted what she said and asked her to explain.

"Why do you think her hubby is sitting up there on the flight deck, Jessica?"

"I'm sure he's qualified," I replied.

"Barely. Wayne arranged for accelerated certification to the 767."

"Why?" I asked, although it struck me that I probably knew the answer.

"Part of the deal with Betsy," Christine said. "Hire me as a flight attendant and my husband as first officer." Christine shook her head. "God, Wayne could be such a pushover when it came to a pretty face and centerfold figure. Betsy got her way, and just in time. She and her hubby have jobs and don't have to put up with their benefactor anymore. How convenient!"

I started to respond, but Christine continued. "It's really very sad, Jessica. I could never understand why Wayne, who was a very bright guy, didn't see through the other women and what they wanted from him. Sure, he was good-looking and had a certain charm, but he was getting older. Did he really think women like Gina and Betsy and God knows how many others climbed into bed with him because he was so sexy? They used him, and he was blind to it. Male ego, I suppose, doing a comb-over to hide the bald spot and pulling in your gut when you look in the mirror."

I could sense that these unpleasant thoughts were eating at Christine. Venting them to me probably provided some relief, but her lower lip began to tremble, and she brushed away a tear that fell to her cheek. Her face turned solemn. "Do you know how many times I wanted to kill Wayne, Jessica?" she said through tightened lips. "Every time I found one of those receipts for a hotel room or piece of jewelry, I wanted to stab him in the heart. I wanted him dead. No, I wanted him to suffer the way I was suffering."

"Why didn't you leave him?" I asked.

"Because—because I decided that living well truly was the best revenge. I'll say this for Wayne. He was as generous to me as he was to his hotties, and I didn't hesitate to take advantage of it. Why do you think I'm fighting so hard for control of SilverAir?

Why would you think I'd join up with Wayne's son, Jason? He's a despicable young man, Jessica. But with that letter Wayne wrote to him, combined with the papers I have, I think we can win the battle with Vicks and Casale."

"Is it really worth it, Christine?"

"I think it is."

Betsy, who'd just taken a call from the flight deck, hung up and came to me. "Captain Caine wonders whether you'd like to come up front, Mrs. Fletcher."

I was torn. I wanted to continue my conversation with Christine. But I had the feeling that she was about to shut down. She'd turned from me, and I could see her reflection in the small window next to her, a sad, bitter face, aging before my eyes.

"I'd love to," I told Betsy.

I looked back to where George was still engrossed in a conversation with Jason. "Will you tell Inspector Sutherland where I've gone?" I asked Betsy.

"Sure."

She tapped on the door to the flight deck in some sort of code. Captain Caine opened it. "Sorry I didn't ask you up for takeoff," he said, "but we were kind of busy."

"I can imagine."

Stepping onto the flight deck of a jetliner at night is like entering a video game of some sort. Outside, there was nothing but blackness. Inside, a hundred tiny lights on the console and above it made me think of Christmas and all the lights on the tree. I started to take the jump seat, but Caine said, "Sit up here," indicating the left-hand chair.

"Oh, I don't think so," I said. "I—"

"No, it's okay. If this weren't a promotional flight, I wouldn't do it. It's more comfortable, gives you a better view." He said to Scherer, "Okay with you, Carl?"

Scherer nodded but said nothing.

Caine helped me into the captain's seat. "Just don't touch anything," he said. "I need to stretch. Back in a few minutes."

He shut the door behind him, leaving me and the first officer on the deathly still flight deck. Scherer ignored me as he inputted information into one of the aircraft's onboard computer systems. I didn't want to say anything to distract him, so I sat quietly, taking everything in with a sense of awe. It was surreal being there, a fairyland high above the Atlantic, winging along at nearly six hundred miles an hour, a hundred or so men and women in the passenger cabin, unaware of the incredible technology and training that went into their safe passage from London to Boston.

After a few minutes of silence, Scherer asked as though querying someone when the next train was due, "You solve the murder yet?"

I didn't say anything for the moment. "I think we're getting close," I said.

"Really? Tell me about it."

"I'd rather have you tell me about it," I said.

"Me? Tell you *what*?"

"What you know. I'm sure you and Captain Caine have discussed it at length."

He'd seemed to tense. Now he relaxed. "Bill? He doesn't talk much about anything. He defines taciturn."

"Yes, I've noticed that. I understand that Wayne Silverton took special pains to have you join SilverAir."

"Where did you hear that?"

"Is it true?"

I could almost hear his mind working.

"That's right," he said. "It worked out pretty good for me."

"So it seems. Mind if I ask why he took such special interest in you?"

"Maybe because he saw that I was a damn good pilot."

"I don't doubt that for a second," I said. "It's just that when someone goes out of his way for another person, it's usually because of some extra-added dimension to that person."

"I'd say ask Wayne, but we know we can't do that, can we?"

"No, unfortunately we can't. How do you feel about your wife working as a flight attendant on the same flight you're piloting?"

"What do you mean?"

"You'll have to forgive me, but I have an insatiable

curiosity about how and why things work. I imagine it makes your life easier having the two of you on the same flight. Come to the airport together, do your work, share a hotel room, and drive home together."

"Yeah, it does have its advantages." He shifted in his seat and looked directly at me. "What are you getting at, Mrs. Fletcher? I get the feeling you're more than just curious."

My sigh said that I agreed with him.

"The inspector from Scotland Yard has already questioned me back in London."

"Yes, he told me he had, and that you were very forthcoming."

"So, let's talk about something more pleasant than Wayne's murder. I'll show you what all these doo-dads do."

He spent the next five minutes instructing me in the layout of the control panels and how the computer system and its autopilot functioned. I enjoyed the brief tutorial and had just thanked him when Captain Caine returned.

"You two getting along okay?" he asked.

"Just fine," I said, getting out of his chair and squeezing against Scherer's shoulder to allow the hefty pilot to resume his seat.

"Thanks," I said. "Captain Scherer showed me how things work up here."

"Ready to take over?" Caine asked.

"Another ten minutes and I might."

When I returned to the passenger cabin, George was sitting next to Seth, who'd awoken and looked fresh as a daisy.

"Everything all right up front?" Seth asked.

"Everything's going fine, smooth as can be."

"Well," said George, "I'd better get back to work. Enjoyed our chat, Doctor."

"Likewise. I think I'll take a little walk. Wouldn't do to come down with a case of deep-vein thrombosis, would it?"

George and I watched Seth start out unsteadily on his stroll around the cabin, gaining stability as he went.

"He's a good man," George said.

"The best," I said. "How did it go with Jason Silverton?"

George smiled. "It occurred to me as we talked that I would like to incarcerate him on general principle. But as far as the murder is concerned, he seems to have a very good alibi. He claims he had dinner that night in an Indian restaurant in London; he showed me the receipt."

"Was he with anyone?"

"He says not."

"He obviously knew his father would be in London. The flight was covered by all the media."

"I'm aware of that. He has no hesitation to say how much he detested his father. It must be dreadful to be hated by your own flesh and blood."

"Wayne may not have been father of the year," I

said, "but Jason's attitude is despicable. Is he a murderer?"

"That remains to be seen. Offhand, I'd say not. How was your visit to the cockpit?"

"They call it a flight deck," I said.

"Of course."

"It was instructive. But even more interesting was the conversation I had with Christine Silverton."

"Let's repair to our private corner where you can tell me all about it."

Chapter Eighteen

I filled George in on my conversation with Christine. He listened intently and without response. When I was finished, he rubbed his nose, raised his eyebrows, and asked, "Your analysis, Jessica?"

"Based upon what she said, members of the crew should top the suspect list."

"That's always been the case, hasn't it?"

"Yes, except there are others—Mr. Casale and Mr. Vicks, and Wayne's son, Jason."

"You're forgetting someone, aren't you?"

"Christine."

"Are you ruling her out after your recent conversation?"

"No. If anyone had a motive to kill Wayne, it was Christine. When I give talks at writers' conferences, I point out that there are basically two reasons to murder. One is in reaction to something, an event, an argument, a long-standing grudge. It generally involves rage or jealousy, and often revenge."

"From what you've learned about her marriage to Mr. Silverton, all those things are present. What's the second motivation?"

"Monetary gain, of course. Greed. A quest for power. Christine stands a good chance of being a part owner of SilverAir. That could be a powerful reason for wanting Wayne out of the way."

"It all adds up to a compelling reason to put her right up there at the top of the list, along with the crew," he said.

"Did Mort speak with you?" I asked.

"Yes. I like him. As he pointed out, having access to the murder weapon is certainly a key to solving this case."

Gina Molnari asked if we wanted a drink or dinner. We passed on both.

"While you're here, Ms. Molnari, I wonder if you'd be good enough to take a short break from your duties and talk with me," George said.

She looked back over the cabin. "I suppose so," she said, "but I'd better ask Christine."

"I'm sure she'll approve," I said. "If you'd like, I'll go mention it to her."

She agreed to that and took a chair across from George.

I went to where Jason and Christine sat together and told her that Gina was being questioned by George.

"Fine," she said.

"I think he thinks I did it," Jason quipped. "Jerk!"

I ignored him and was about to rejoin George when the muffled sound of a weapon being discharged came from the direction of the flight deck.

"What was that?" Christine said, sitting up ramrod straight.

"It sounded like a gunshot," I said.

The plane suddenly lurched hard to the right, causing those standing to fall against other passengers, or over seat backs. It then righted itself and banked to the left, reversing the mayhem in the aisles.

"What's going on?" someone yelled.

"Are we going to crash?" the Boston councilwoman shrieked.

We were flying straight and level again. Christine stood and said, "I'd better see what's happening up front." She turned to Betsy Scherer. "Knock on the door."

Betsy did as instructed. There was no response.

"Do you have a key?" Christine asked. I would have been surprised if she had one. One of many security measures put into place on commercial aircraft was to deny flight attendants a key to the flight deck to preclude the possibility of one of them being held hostage and forced to give it up to a terrorist.

"Gina has one. She always keeps it on her."

So much for following security regulations.

"Then go get it!" Christine snapped.

Betsy returned with Gina, and the key to the flight deck, which Betsy used to open the door. The sight shocked our small group into frozen silence. Captain

Caine lay on the floor on his stomach, his feet between the twin seats, his head at the flight deck's threshold.

"Oh, my God," Christine said, her hand to her mouth.

Caine managed to turn on his side, exposing a dark circle of blood on his white uniform shirt, just below his sternum. He pressed an open hand against it and looked up at us.

"Bill," Gina said, falling to her knees and touching his face.

I looked past them into the cockpit. Carl Scherer had twisted in his chair and stared at me. His expression was vacant, almost like someone in a coma. And he held an automatic weapon in his right hand.

Seth had come forward.

"Help him," Gina pleaded. "Oh, my God, someone please help him."

"Bring him out," Seth said, aware that Scherer's weapon was pointed in our direction.

George and the male flight attendant, John Slater, grabbed Caine beneath his arms and slid him out of the cockpit to the carpet just outside the door.

"Hey," Mort said to Scherer, "put that gun down."

Scherer's reply was to motion for Betsy to come to him.

"Don't," I told her.

"Betsy, I need you," Scherer said in a voice that verged upon cracking.

"Please," I said through the open door, "put down

the gun. You have a plane full of innocent people. Don't compound what's already happened."

"Betsy!" he commanded, his voice stronger now.

She looked to me. I shook my head and again said to her husband, "I'm pleading with you to be sensible, Mr. Scherer. Put down the weapon and come out here."

George was at my side again. "Don't make a bad situation worse," he added.

Betsy said nothing as she entered the cockpit and closed the door behind her, taking the key to the flight deck door with her.

We looked at each other, aware of the ramifications facing us.

Seth and Mort had dragged Caine to a bulkhead where there was room for Seth to administer to the wound. He tore open the pilot's shirt, grunted in response to what he saw, looked up, and said, "I need a clean towel, and make it quick!"

Gina fetched one and handed it to him. He pressed it against Caine's stomach. "I presume you have a first aid kit aboard," he said sternly. Gina got that for him, too, and Seth used items from it to help stabilize Caine and to make him more comfortable. He stood and came to me, whispering in my ear, "He's not in good shape, Jessica. We've got to get him to a hospital."

"Scherer's in command of the flight," George said, glumly.

"I'm afraid so."

Jed joined us. "That nut is still up front?"

"Yes."

"Can't anyone talk sense into him?"

"I tried," I said.

"Did the captain say anything?" Jed asked.

"No."

Jed repeated the question to Seth.

"He says he tried to take the weapon from the first officer, and it went off in the struggle," Seth reported.

"Why did he pull it out in the first place?" Mort asked. He'd retrieved his handgun from his carry-on bag and had slipped it into his waistband.

"The only important thing now," Jed said, "is to get control of the aircraft."

"We can bust through the door," Mort said.

"Bad idea," Jed countered. "The doors have been reinforced since Nine Eleven. Besides, he can send us into a spin we'll never recover from. He has that flight attendant with him."

"His wife."

Seth returned to Caine's side, and we stood over them.

"Can you talk?" Jed asked.

Caine looked up, grimaced against his pain, and said, "Yeah. A little."

"Not too long," Seth cautioned.

"We're on autopilot, right?" Jed said.

Caine nodded.

"Is he capable of deliberately crashing us?" Jed asked. "Mentally?"

"I—I think he is," was Caine's reply.

Christine gasped.

"We've got to get inside that cockpit," Mort said.

No one offered any solutions to the obvious.

"We'll just have to wait him out," Christine said.

Jason, who'd remained in his seat throughout what had transpired, now joined us.

"Are we going to die?" he asked no one in particular.

I asked Gina, "Can I speak with Officer Scherer over the internal phone system?"

"Sure."

"Set it up for me."

She went to the cabin phone hanging on the wall just outside the flight deck and dialed in a number. She handed the phone to me.

"Captain Scherer?" I said.

There was no reply.

"Captain Scherer, this is Jessica Fletcher. I'm sure you can explain what's happened, and I'm also certain that you'll receive a fair hearing. You're a professional, a highly trained and skilled commercial airline pilot. I know that you put the safety and well-being of your passengers first and foremost. I have tremendous respect for what you do, and so do the others standing here with me. Dr. Hazlitt has tended to Captain Caine's wounds, but unless we get him to a hospital quickly, he might not make it. You don't want that on your conscience, Captain. I know you don't."

I waited.

I shook my head and looked for input from those near me. They had nothing to offer.

"Let me try," Jed said, taking the phone from me. "Captain Scherer? This is Jed Richardson. I used to sit in that same seat you're in, sir. We share a bond as professional pilots, one based upon the trust our passengers place in us. The men and women in this passenger cabin are counting on you to get them safely down to the ground. Your colleague, Captain Caine, needs immediate medical help. How about letting me come up front with you and give you a hand in getting this bird to Boston? We can't be more than an hour from there. How about it?"

"Leave me alone," Scherer said.

Jed placed his hand over the mouthpiece and repeated to us what Scherer had said. His voice could be heard again, and Jed returned the phone to his ear. "What's that you say, Captain?"

Jed handed the phone to me. "He wants to talk to you, Jess."

"This is Jessica Fletcher," I said. "I'm listening."

"Maybe you'll understand," he said.

"Understand what?"

"What happened to Wayne Silverton."

"I'll certainly try," I said. "Will you let me come in with you? I promise I'll be the only one. We can discuss whatever you'd like."

A female voice came through the phone from the flight deck. "Carl, please," Betsy Scherer said. "We can work this out. Please!"

The phone went dead. I put it in its cradle. "He hung up," I announced.

"We'll just have to wait him out and hope for the best," Mort said.

"That's not good enough, Mort," Jed said.

I was aware that everyone on the flight had come to the front of the cabin and was jammed together, attempting to learn what was transpiring. I said to Christine, "Someone had better pass along some information before we have hysteria."

She got on the PA. "Ladies and gentlemen, you're all aware that there's been an accident on the flight deck. Captain Caine has been injured, but Dr. Hazlitt is taking good care of him. Captain Scherer is in command of the flight now, and we're proceeding as scheduled to Boston. Please, I ask everyone to return to your seats and fasten your seat belts in the event we should encounter clear-air turbulence."

Gina Molnari approached the crowd and urged them toward the rear of the aircraft, deflecting their anxious questions in a clear, calm voice. "Everything will be just fine," she repeated over and over. "Everyone stay calm, and we'll be in Boston before we know it."

Jed moved us to one of the galleys. "Look," he said, "chances are he's not about to kill himself by crashing the aircraft. We'll have to do what Mort said, wait him out. But we'd better have a contingency plan in the event we have to physically take control of the plane. You're armed, Mort. Right?"

Mort patted the weapon in his waistband.

"You?" Jed asked George.

"Afraid not," George said.

"If my calculations are correct," Jed said, "we're about forty-five minutes from Boston."

"Can you fly this plane?" Mort asked.

"I haven't flown a 767 before, but it's not all that different from the 757. Boeing designed the 767 to be flown by 757 pilots with a minimum of training."

"That's good to hear," Jim Shevlin said. He'd come from the rear of the plane and stood in the galley entrance.

"Do you think he'd listen to me?" Christine asked. "You know, as the airline's owner?"

"Sounds to me like Jess or Jed has the best chance of getting through to him," said Mort.

"Here's what we should be prepared to do," Jed said. "In the event there's a change in the flight, I suggest we—"

We all stood a little straighter as there was a discernible change in the aircraft's motion. Jed cocked his head and frowned. "We're turning," he said. "He's off the autopilot. We're heading back to sea."

Chapter Nineteen

Jed got on the phone. "Mr. Scherer, this is Jed Richardson. Why have you come off autopilot?"

Scherer said nothing.

"What's your fuel?" Jed asked.

Again, no response.

Then Scherer said, "I'd like to talk to Mrs. Fletcher."

"He wants you, Jess," Jed said, handing me the phone.

"This is Jessica."

"I want to talk to you, explain things."

"Of course. What is it you want to say?"

"Come up here."

"To the flight deck?"

"Yeah."

I told George and Jed what Scherer wanted.

"Absolutely not," George said. "He's already shot one person."

"We'd better do something," Jed said, "and fast!"

"I'll do what he wants," I said.

"Jessica, I—"

"It'll be all right, George. Jed is right. We can't simply stand by and wait for him to run out of fuel and kill us all. I'll be fine."

"All right," George said, "but only ten minutes— and no more." He turned to Jed: "I know these cockpit doors have been strengthened since Nine Eleven, but surely they can be battered open if enough force is applied."

"We can try," Jed said.

"Mrs. F.," Mort said, "I've got an idea. Maybe after you go in you can close the door, but not tight."

"I can try," I said.

"Chances are he won't notice," Mort added. "Will it stay closed that way, Jed, or will it swing open?"

"It'll stay where you leave it," Jed replied.

"Good," I said. To Gina: "Betsy has the key, can you signal them inside to open the door?"

She nodded, and rapped out a code on the door with her knuckles.

I pushed open the door and saw Betsy Scherer standing behind her husband, her hands on his shoulders.

"He's asked for me," I told her.

She replied by walking past me to where the others waited in the passenger cabin.

I took a final look at George before stepping onto

the flight deck. I waited a moment, then slowly closed the door behind me, careful not to go so far as to cause it to latch.

Scherer didn't look back at me.

"Mr. Scherer?" I said. "May I call you Captain Scherer?"

He turned his head slightly. "Call me what you want. Go on, take the left seat."

"I'm comfortable standing," I said.

He turned the control yoke to the right, causing the right wing to dip, and the left wing to come up, sending us into a hard right turn and sending me up against a control panel. "Sit down," he said after he'd leveled off.

I slid into the seat reserved for a flight's captain and peered into the night through the windshield. My eyes located the compass. It read ninety degrees. Jed was right; we were heading east again, back over the Atlantic.

"You said you wanted to explain what happened to Wayne Silverton," I said in a soft voice, not wanting to arouse him, but also aware that I was on a ten-minute leash.

"Silverton deserved to die," he said, his eyes never leaving the console in front of him, his hands gripping the yoke. The handgun he'd used to shoot Bill Caine rested on his lap.

"Why?" I asked.

"Ask his wife."

"I'm asking you, Captain."

"The way he treated Betsy. The way he treated everybody."

"What did he do to Betsy?"

"He treated her like one of his whores."

What ran through my mind at the moment was not especially kind. Evidently, Betsy had provided Wayne sexual favors in return for something tangible, in this case a job for her and her husband. That's as good a definition of prostitution as any.

"I'm sorry to hear that," I said. "It must have been hurtful for you to watch that happening to the woman you love. But why did you agree to come to work for Wayne and SilverAir?"

It was the first time he looked directly at me. "Do you know what it's like to be a junior pilot in the airline business these days, Mrs. Fletcher?"

"I'm afraid I don't."

"It stinks. I flew regional jets from one Podunk town to another. Know how much I was paid for putting in fourteen-hour days, making a dozen tough landings and takeoffs every day? Twenty-eight thousand. That was it."

"But you knew you could eventually advance to bigger and better things."

"Bigger and better things? In this aviation climate? Pilots with tons more seniority and experience than me are being laid off right and left. Silverton offered me a dream job, right seat in a 767, with the possibility of the left seat pretty soon. I grabbed it, only I figured once Betsy and I were working for him, he'd lay off her. He was a slimeball. He was all over her, always reminding her that he could fire us as fast as he'd hired us."

He'd been sitting straight while condemning Wayne. Now, as though the air had left him, he slumped back in the seat and began to weep, softly at first, then with more passion.

I eyed the weapon on his lap. Did I dare reach for it? He'd showed me the fuel gauges during my previous trip to the flight deck. I didn't know exactly what the digital numbers represented, but they appeared to indicate we didn't have much left.

"We're not heading for Boston any longer, are we?" I said.

He stared through the windshield at the black void outside.

My ten minutes were ticking away.

"Will you give me the gun, Carl?" I said.

He placed his hand on it, and for a terrible moment I thought he might slip his finger onto the trigger and use it on me. Instead, he handed it across the divide between our seats.

"Thank you," I said.

I struggled out of the confined seat, went to the door, and pulled it open. George, Mort, Christine, Jed, Jim Shevlin, Gina Molnari, and John Slater stood waiting. I handed the gun to George.

"Better take him out of there, Inspector," Jed said, "before he decides to do something really crazy."

There was no need to enter the cockpit and forcibly

remove him. He'd put the aircraft on autopilot again, had risen from his seat, and walked into our midst.

"You're under arrest for the murder of Wayne Silverton," George said.

"I'll take him," Mort said, leading Scherer to a pair of seats not far away, his weapon trained at the pilot's head. Once there, Mort pulled Scherer's arms behind him and secured them with duct tape provided by Slater from the aircraft's supply of emergency repair items.

"I'd better climb in that left seat," Jed said, "and get this bird headed in the right direction. Come help me out, Jess."

"Me?"

"Yup. Get in the right seat. I'll be plenty busy and may need you to lend a hand at times."

Chapter Twenty

Before accompanying Jed to the flight deck, I asked if George could take the jump seat, and Jed agreed.

"Let's get this sucker back on course," Jed said once he was settled and had familiarized himself with where everything was located. "Why don't you two put on your headsets and hear what's going on."

He turned the 767 back to a westerly heading, in the direction of Boston, and made radio contact with the appropriate air traffic centers, informing them of our situation, and requesting that an ambulance be there when we arrived, as well as law enforcement officers to take an alleged murderer into custody. The controller assured Jed that we would be given priority landing rights.

"How's our fuel?" I asked.

"I'd like to have more of a cushion," he said, "but we should be all right as long as we don't have delays at Logan."

As we bore through the night sky toward Boston,

it became obvious that my presence wasn't needed. I suppose Jed wanted company, which I was happy to provide. I looked back often at George, who seemed enthralled at the experience of being on the flight deck of a sophisticated jet airliner. No matter how worldly someone might be, the experience was bound to impress.

After some back-and-forth over the radio between Jed and the air traffic control people in the Boston area, we settled into the approach procedure for Logan International Airport. Jed's professionalism was obvious. He flew the plane as though he'd been doing it every day of his life. He hadn't flown commercial jets in a number of years, but I suppose it's like falling off a bicycle, as the saying goes. He was supremely confident and very much in command.

We eventually entered the traffic pattern and Jed lowered the landing gear. "Uh oh," he said.

George and I leaned closer to him.

"See that light?" he said, pointing to the console.

"Which one?" I asked.

He touched it with his finger.

"It's off," I said.

"Should be on," he said.

"That's the light that malfunctioned when we were leaving Boston," I commented.

"The gear is down," Jed said, "but that light is supposed to come on to indicate it's locked in place."

"Maybe the bulb is burnt-out," George offered, hopefully.

"And maybe it's not," Jed growled. He got back on the radio and reported the problem to Boston Approach Control. The controller asked Jed how much fuel he was carrying.

"We're light," Jed responded.

"Want to do a pass for a visual?" asked the controller.

"Roger," Jed said crisply. "Shall do."

Jed told us, "I'm going to do a flyby of the tower. They'll visually confirm whether the gear looks like it's down all the way."

"That sounds sensible," George said.

"Doesn't mean it's locked, though," Jed warned. "If it's not, it'll collapse when we land."

The controller on the ground informed Jed that other traffic had been cleared from airspace surrounding the airport, and we were okay to make the tower pass. The airport and all its lights came into view as we broke through a layer of low clouds. The closer we got to the ground, the faster the aircraft seemed to be flying. Jed kept dropping our altitude until we were headed directly at the control tower. I doubted whether we were more than five hundred feet from the ground. A powerful searchlight on the tower sprung to life, and its operator trained it on our plane. I wondered for a moment whether we were too low and would crash into the tower. But Jed maneuvered the 767 so that it passed a few hundred feet above, and to the south of it.

"Gear is down, Captain," the controller's voice barked into our headsets.

"Roger," Jed replied. "Clear us for landing."

"You're cleared, SilverAir."

We climbed to the right altitude for a straight-in approach to Runway Four-Right, one of Logan's longest runways. As Jed coaxed the aircraft into the prescribed landing configuration and attitude, he got on the intercom: "Ladies and gentlemen, we've got a minor problem with the aircraft. Nothing to worry about, but better safe than sorry. Please see that your seat belts are securely fastened and that any loose objects are stowed. Please remove your glasses, if you wear them. Women should remove shoes with high heels. The flight attendants will show you the proper position to assume for landing."

Gina Molnari called the flight deck, and Jed informed her of the situation. "Keep everybody calm back there," he instructed.

"Shall do, Captain," she responded crisply.

The runway was clearly visible, and we could see emergency vehicles racing down the runway, creating a kaleidoscopic, flashing light show.

"All set?" Jed asked us.

"Yes, sir," George said.

"Yes, sir," I said.

"Then let's do it!"

Jed drained off altitude and airspeed as we approached the runway's threshold. Soon, we were over it, and the moment of truth had arrived. Would the gear hold up? Or would we end up on the 767's belly, sliding crazily down the runway until inertia brought us to a natural stop, hopefully without serious injury to the plane and passengers? That many of the emergency vehicles standing at the ready were fire engines reminded everyone that fire was the most serious of possible outcomes.

The wheels touched, came back up off the runway, touched again, and this time stayed down, solid and sure. The faint sound of applause from the passenger cabin drifted through the flight deck door.

I breathed a deep, prolonged sigh of relief. I looked back at George, who gave me a warm smile and a sharp nod of his head. "Well done, Captain," he said as Jed taxied the jet to its assigned spot on the airport. Because we'd landed in emergency status, we weren't allowed to park at the terminal. Instead, we were directed to a relatively secluded area and were told that a set of mobile stairs would be brought for deplaning. Buses would transport everyone to the terminal.

Once inside, we were herded into a large room and instructed by uniformed officers that we'd have to stay there until further notice. We weren't the usual group of arriving passengers. Ours was not a scheduled flight; customs clearances had to be arranged outside normal channels. Also, our captain had been shot by the first officer and required swift medical attention. An ambulance had whisked him off to an area hospital, and Seth reported that he was confident Captain Caine would survive. His assailant, First Officer Carl Scherer, was taken to a holding cell at the airport and would remain there until the complex questions of jurisdiction were sorted out.

"Quite a ride," George said to me when he returned from a meeting with local and state law enforcement authorities.

"Thank goodness Jed was along. What would we have done without him?"

"I have the feeling you could have landed us safely, Jessica."

I laughed. "Your faith is grossly misplaced, George. But thanks for the vote of confidence."

I thought of those motion pictures in which an untrained pilot is forced to fly a commercial jetliner after a catastrophe has felled the regular pilots. Usually, those screen heroines were flight attendants. The notion that I might have been forced to sit in the 767's left-hand seat and get us safely on the ground in Boston was ludicrous. But I would have tried if called upon. I shuddered at the thought.

"Well, George," I said, "you got your man."

"Through no effort on my part."

I looked out over the assembled passengers and spotted the three flight attendants, Gina, Betsy, and John, standing apart from the rest.

"I wonder—"

George turned. "Wonder what, Jessica?"

"I wonder whether the plane had a cockpit voice recorder."

"Ask our pilot over there," George said, pointing to Jed Richardson, who was surrounded by passengers thanking him for having saved us.

I went to Jed and waited for a break in the congratulations being heaped upon him. "Jed," I said, "I assume the plane has a cockpit voice recorder."

"Sure it does," he said. "Federal regulations. One of two black boxes on every flight."

"Was it turned on?"

"You bet it was, from the minute the engines were started at Stansted. It can't be turned off by the crew. That would defeat the whole purpose of it."

"When can we hear it?"

"I don't understand."

"Carl Scherer and his wife spent considerable time together alone on the flight deck. I'd like to know what they talked about."

"I doubt if the authorities would release the tape to you, Jess. Cockpit conversations are confidential unless they're used in an accident investigation by the National Transportation Safety Board."

"Even in a murder investigation?"

"Hmmm. Let me ask the right people."

George returned from his latest meeting as Jed left in search of an aviation authority.

"We're still squabbling over what to do with Mr. Scherer," George said. "The FBI was called in, so we have your city and airport police, the FBI, and of course, Scotland Yard represented by yours truly."

I told him what I'd asked Jed to do regarding the cockpit voice recorder.

"Interesting idea, Jessica. That tape will undoubtedly prove useful to the prosecution during Scherer's trial."

"Or the defense," I said.

"How so?"

"I'm not sure, George. I just know I'd like to hear what they said to each other."

A few minutes later, Jed came back. "They'll do it, Jess," he said, "provided the request comes from an official law enforcement source." He smiled. "I asked them if Scotland Yard qualifies. They said they thought so. Come with me, Inspector. They want to talk to you. In the meantime, they're removing the black boxes from the aircraft. NTSB has a lab unit here at Logan. They can run the tape for us in there."

By this time, the rest of the passengers were on edge, and that's being kind. Some had become downright surly at being detained, and no matter how many times officers assigned to keep us in a group explained the necessity of it, tempers weren't salved. Churlson Vicks and Sal Casale were especially vocal. "We own this bloody airline," Vicks commanded in a loud voice. "I demand that we be allowed to go."

Christine Silverton made similar protestations but in a more subdued manner. Her stepson, Jason, sat brooding on a folding chair in a corner of the room.

A few members of the press threatened an exposé if they weren't allowed to leave immediately. The look on the officers' faces said plainly that they'd heard it all before and didn't care one iota about exposés.

It took a half hour for the tape from the flight deck to be removed from the black box, which was actually red, and to have it ready to roll on NTSB playback equipment. I joined George and a contingent of other law enforcement officers in the small room, and we took chairs arranged in a semicircle around the table on which the playback unit sat.

"Ready?" a technician asked.

"Let her roll," an FBI agent said.

"I've fast-forwarded to the section you said you were interested in," said the tech. "It begins with, 'Betsy, I need you.'"

"Good."

The speakers erupted with sound, and the technician adjusted the volume to a more reasonable level. *"Betsy, I need you,"* was heard, along with muffled voices recorded from a distance, obviously belonging to us as we stood outside the cockpit and pleaded with Scherer to put down his weapon.

The sound of the flight deck door closing was unmistakable.

"Carl, what are you doing?" It was Betsy's voice.

"I'm going to take us down," Carl said.

"Are you crazy?" she said, panic in her voice. *"Why did you shoot Bill?"*

"He knew."

"Knew what?"

"About Wayne. He accused me of taking his knife from his case and—" His next words were garbled.

"And you shot him?"

"I didn't mean to. I pulled out the gun to scare him off, but he jumped on me. It just went off. I swear. I know it's over, Betsy."

"Carl, we can get through this. Bill's not dead. Tell everybody it was a mistake, an accident; they'll let you fly the plane to Boston. After that, we can—" We couldn't make out the rest of what she said.

"No matter what happens, Betsy, I'll never let you go to jail. I swear I won't. I'd rather go down in the Atlantic than see that happen."

"No one has to go to jail, Carl. For God's sake, stop this!"

"I know why you killed Wayne, Betsy. He deserved it, damn it! You did what you had to do to get him off your back. He was scum!"

She was heard crying.

"Please don't kill us all," she pleaded.

A long period transpired during which no words were spoken. There were the sounds of Betsy's sobbing, and at one point we heard her say, "I love you."

Eventually, the tape reached the point when Scherer agreed to allow me to come to the flight deck, and I replaced Betsy.

"You can turn it off now," I said. "We know the rest."

Chapter Twenty-one

The mood was somber during the trip from Boston to Cabot Cove. The events of the past few days had settled in on all of us, and the realization that we came close to meeting a cold, violent death in the Atlantic Ocean wasn't far from anyone's thoughts.

I'd convinced George to spend a few days in Cabot Cove, and he'd received permission from his superiors in London to do just that.

"It was heartbreaking to see that lovely young flight attendant led away in handcuffs," Susan Shevlin said as our stretch limo brought us closer to home.

"Husband and wife hauled off that way," Seth added, sadly. "They sold their souls to the devil, who in this case turned out to be Wayne Silverton."

"They'll both spend the majority of their lives behind bars," said Mort, "her for murdering Wayne, him for—all sorts of charges will be leveled at him."

"Captain Caine was almost another victim," I said.

"I checked with the hospital just before we left," Seth said. "He'll pull through fine."

"Thanks to you, Doc," Mort said.

"Thanks to Jessica, we *all* pulled through," Maureen Metzger said, her voice breaking.

"Let's not forget Jed," Jim Shevlin said.

"Amen!"

Jed and Barbara Richardson had flown to Boston in one of his two-seater Cessna 172s, and had left Logan Airport in it for the return trip to Cabot Cove. Jed's final words to us were, "If we don't make it, it's because we're overweight from all the stuff Barbara bought."

"How did you know that it was the first officer's wife who'd stabbed Wayne Silverton," George asked, "and not him?"

"I didn't know," I said. "I just had this gut feeling. If he'd wanted to kill Wayne, he would have used the handgun he carried with him, not stolen Caine's knife for the task. Besides, it was Betsy who'd been directly on the receiving end of his advances. If it weren't for the cockpit voice recorder, we'd never have known. I'm sure Mr. Scherer would have maintained that he'd killed Wayne in order to save her."

"At least there was some honor to the whole sordid mess," was Seth's comment.

Talk naturally turned to Christine Silverton. "What do you think will happen with her?" Maureen asked.

"That's up to the lawyers and the courts," I said. I managed a laugh. "As we were leaving, I heard

Mr. Casale say to Mr. Vicks that he was selling his share of SilverAir to the first sucker that came along. That's exactly the way he put it. But I think that if whoever ends up owning it can get past this rocky start, it has a good chance of succeeding. All the drama aside, it was a good flight. Wayne was right. People will be willing to pay a little extra for some comfort and decent service."

"Sounds like you're getting ready to apply to SilverAir for a job as a stewardess, Jessica," Seth quipped.

"The last thing I'd want to do," I said. "I'm too old. And they're not called stewardesses anymore, not with so many men holding those jobs."

"There's no age restriction on being a flight attendant anymore," Jim Shevlin said.

"That doesn't matter," I said. "Besides, I'm not about to be asking, 'Coffee, tea, or me?' of anyone." I turned and looked at George, who'd said little during the long drive. He smiled and patted my knee.

George stayed in one of Seth's spare rooms, and we all met for breakfast at Mara's the following morning. Everyone looked rested and moods were considerably lighter than the night before. Other people in the dockside eatery knew of our adventure through television reports from Boston. Naturally, there were many questions, including a flurry of them by two reporters from Cabot Cove's daily newspaper who'd tracked us down that morning. We decided to elect one spokesman to speak for us all, and that person was Mayor Jim Shevlin, who promised the reporters he'd meet with them later that morning.

"What's on your agenda today?" Maureen Metzger asked after we'd consumed stacks of Mara's famed blueberry pancakes, and plenty of her strong coffee.

"I thought I'd go flying for an hour."

"How could you possibly even think of doing that after what we went through yesterday?" Maureen asked.

"It's the most relaxing thing I can think of," I said.

"Mind a passenger?" George asked.

"I'd love one."

"You're brave to fly with me," I said to George, who sat in the right-hand seat of the Cessna 172 aircraft I'd rented for an hour from Jed Richardson's flight service. "I don't have much experience."

"Knowing how capable and responsible you are with everything else you tackle, Jessica, I'm sure flying isn't an exception."

We took a leisurely flight over the area surrounding the town, and I pointed out landmarks that I'd become familiar with during my flight training with Jed. I ended up flying over Cabot Cove itself so he could see it from the air.

"As lovely as from the ground," he commented after I announced it was time to return the plane. I made a slow turn in the direction of the airport.

"Well, Jessica, you seem to be supremely relaxed up here in control of your airplane."

"I am," I agreed. "I don't think I've ever experienced such a feeling of freedom and relaxation before. Everyone kids me, of course. I fly a plane but don't drive a car."

"From the statistics you've cited to me, we're considerably safer up here than down there on a highway."

"It's more than that," I said as the airport came into sight. It takes time for novice pilots to be able to pick out runways from a few thousand feet above the earth, but you eventually become skilled at it. "The world disappears when I'm flying. My biggest regret is not having more time to enjoy it."

"You're a busy woman, Jessica Fletcher," he said, a hint of sadness in his voice. "You fly. You write bestselling novels. You tend your garden and cook elaborate meals and travel the world and—"

"I can't ever imagine not being busy," I said while trimming up the plane with the small trim tab wheel on the floor between our seats.

"Would you ever consider slowing down a bit and moving to London?"

"I've thought of that many times, George. It's one of my favorite cities in the world, and knowing you're there only enhances the concept."

"Well?"

I shook my head and added a little more throttle

to maintain altitude. "It's just not in the cards for me, I'm afraid, at least not at this juncture."

He laughed. "Recently, I've wondered whether I could be happy living in—oh, let's say, the States. I'm coming up on retirememt age and—"

"You? Retired? I can't imagine it. You'd be bored silly."

"You're probably right, although the notion has a certain appeal. I wonder how good friends living an ocean apart managed to see each other now and then before the aircraft was invented, or fast steamships."

"I'm sure they managed," I said.

"Just as we manage."

"Yes," I agreed with a smile. "Just as we manage."

We fell silent and focused on the sights two thousand feet below.

"I feel sorry for the flight attendant, Ms. Molnari," he said as I banked the plane into a shallow turn. "She had her nasty little fling with Silverton but fell madly in love with Captain Caine. She told me when I interviewed her during the flight to Boston that Caine was insanely jealous of Silverton and of her affair with him, as brief as it might have been. Caine threatened to break off their relationship. That's why she feigned her suicide attempt, an ill-advised grandstand play to get his attention."

"With Christine Silverton's sleeping pills."

"Yes. Unknown to Mrs. Silverton, Caine had announced to Ms. Molnari that he was ending their relationship. He was in the enviable—or perhaps unenviable—position of having two attractive women in love with him. Ms. Molnari and Mrs. Silverton. Shortly after being told by Caine that he was breaking it off, Molnari was berated by Mrs. Silverton in her hotel room for having stolen Caine from her. This twin assault was too much for Ms. Molnari. She grabbed the bottle of sleeping pills from Mrs. Silverton's bathroom, returned to Caine's room, and swallowed some of the pills in his presence. Foolish woman."

" 'Desperate' is more apt," I said.

"I suppose you're right. The reason she didn't accompany the rest of the crew into London the night you arrived was that she and Caine had a few drinks at Stansted. I don't believe there ever was an old flying buddy, as he claimed."

"We both knew that, George, without being told. Time to go back." I started the process of setting up to enter the traffic pattern at the Cabot Cove airport.

"Yes, time to go back," he said. "I wish it weren't the case."

"I've only rented the plane for an hour."

"I wasn't talking about going back to the airport, Jessica. I meant having to go back to London tomorrow. I like it here."

"And I love having you here."

"Maybe one day we'll find time to *really* get to know each other, time together without a bloody murder interfering."

272

I laughed. "Based upon my track record, George, that's not very likely. But I share your sentiment. Let's make a point of it."

I entered Cabot Cove Airport's left-hand traffic pattern, the standard for most airports unless otherwise posted, flew the downwind leg with the wind behind me, turned onto what's called the base leg, and then made another ninety-degree left turn that lined me up with the twenty-one-hundred-foot asphalt runway. Every pilot knows that a perfect landing isn't possible every time, no matter how skilled and experienced you are, but I wanted this one to be as smooth as possible. It turned out to be just that, a by-the-book touchdown at precisely the point on the runway I'd aimed for. I turned off the runway as soon as the small plane had slowed sufficiently and taxied to the hangar where Jed housed and maintained his fleet of small planes. He waved as I pulled up to the tie-down area and killed the engine.

"Bravo, Jessica," George said.

He leaned over and kissed my cheek. "Next thing I know," he said, "you'll be applying to become an astronaut."

"I'd take you with me to the moon," I said.

"And I wouldn't hesitate to go."

"**Y**ou must be beside yourself with worry," I said.

"I haven't slept a wink since I received the call from the Alaska State Police."

"She's disappeared? I mean, *really* disappeared?"

"Yes. At least that's what the police said. She left the ship in Ketchikan and never returned. They have a system for tracking people who get off the ship to enjoy shore time in the ports. They scan your passenger card when you leave the ship, and again when you return. Their computers show her leaving at nine-thirty in the morning, but she was never scanned as having returned."

"Maybe their computers made a mistake," Seth Hazlitt said. My dear friend, and Cabot Cove's most popular physician, has an inherent mistrust of computers.

We were gathered in my living room. It had been a particularly cold March, with a series of snowstorms, and many days when the temperature never rose above freezing. I'd made stew, whipped up a salad, and served a red wine recommended to me by my favorite Cabot Cove wine shop. After dinner, we retreated to my living room, where I had the fireplace going, and I served cof-

fee and tea, and a plate of cookies. With me were Seth;
Sheriff Mort Metzger and his wife, Maureen; Charlene
Sassi, owner of the town's favorite bakery and the source
of the cookies; Michael Cunniff, one of Cabot Cove's
leading attorneys; and Kathy Copeland, a dear friend of
many years and the person relating this troublesome
tale. She'd received the call about her sister five days
earlier, and had immediately flown to Alaska to confer
with authorities there. She'd returned to Cabot Cove
only yesterday.

"I spoke with that officer in Alaska," Mort said.
"They seem like competent fellas."

"I'm sure they are," I agreed.

"Very nice and very professional," Kathy said. "And
I appreciate you taking the time to speak with them,
Mort."

"Least I could do," our sheriff replied.

"Kathy, I don't want to make light of your concern," I
said, "but your sister, Wilimena, has been known in the
past to—well, to disappear for periods of time."

Kathy sat back in her chair, rolled her eyes, and sighed.
"I know, I know," she said. "Willie has always been a free
spirit. There have been times when I wasn't able to reach
her for months at a stretch, but then she surfaced from
wherever she'd gone and regaled me with tales of her adventures. But this feels different."

She sat up straight and extended her hands as though
to elicit our understanding and agreement with what she
was about to say. "There was no reason for her to leave
the ship and not come back. Sure, Willie would take off
at the drop of a hat and follow some whim of the moment, but not this way. I just know something terrible
has happened to her."

We fell silent as we contemplated what she'd said, and
avoided further comment by taking much longer than
necessary to choose a cookie from the platter. Mort
broke the silence.

"You say you brought back some of her things," he
said to Kathy.

"Yes. The cruise authorities sealed off her cabin and secured all of her personal belongings."

"Did the Alaskan police examine those things?" I asked.

"Some of them, Jessica. Willie always took along a large envelope in which to keep her receipts from a trip. The police photocopied them for me."

"Those receipts would give some indication of where she went, and what she might have done in the various ports-of-call," I offered.

"Did you look through them yourself?" Michael Cunniff asked. He had been practicing law in Cabot Cove for as long as I've lived there. He was in his late seventies but hadn't lost a step mentally. Physically, however, he was a mass of orthopedic maladies, which necessitated walking with a cane. With long, flowing silver hair and a penchant for colorful bow ties to accompany his many suits, he was an attorney out of central casting—or maybe a United States senator of yesteryear.

"I must have gone over them a dozen times on the flight home," Kathy replied, referring to her sister's receipts. "They were all from the ports the ship had visited earlier, Juneau and Sitka. Ketchikan was the last stop in Alaska before returning to Seattle."

"And?" I asked.

Kathy shrugged. "They mean nothing to me. Just receipts from shops and restaurants Willie visited in those ports, and a bunch of shipboard receipts, too, from the various lounges and shops."

"I'd like to see them," Michael said. He'd been Kathy's attorney since she moved to Cabot Cove forty years ago.

"Of course," she said.

"Are the Alaskan police at all confident about finding Wilimena?" Seth asked.

"They said they would do all they could," Kathy answered, "but they also reminded me that Alaska is a very big place . . . especially—"

"Especially what?" I asked.

"Especially if Willie doesn't want to be found."

"Ironic, isn't it, Jess, that you'll soon be heading for Alaska?" Maureen said.

It was true. I'd visited our forty-ninth state years ago on a whirlwind book promotion tour. So, although I literally had visited Alaska, I'd never seen it, and had decided to rectify that by booking an Inland Passage cruise—the same one Kathy's sister, Wilimena, had taken and from which she'd vanished. I'd booked the cruise months in advance, combining it with a long weekend in Seattle prior to the ship's departure. I have a favorite mystery bookstore there run by a marvelous gentleman, Bill Farley, who always arranges for a book signing whenever I'm within striking distance of his store on Cherry Street.

My reason for choosing an Alaskan cruise, as opposed to visiting other places on the globe, was a nagging need to get closer to nature. It had been building in me all winter, and by the time January rolled around, it had become almost an obsession. True, Maine teems with wildlife, which is one of many reasons I love living there. But Alaska has a very different lure for those of us enamored of nature and the remarkable array of creatures with whom we share our planet. So many of my friends have returned from up north filled with lifelong memories of having sailed into the midst of a pod of orca whales, or having seen majestic bald eagles on virtually every treetop. Witnessing nature up close and personal has always helped me put things, including myself, into perspective, affirming my place in this world.

"Maybe you could ask a few questions while you're there, Mrs. F.," Mort suggested. "You know, check in with the local police and see if they've made any progress in finding Wilimena."

"I'd be happy to do that," I said, "although I'm not sure they'd be anxious to share anything with me."

"But they would with me," Kathy said.

"Of course they would," said Mort. "You're the missing person's sister."

Kathy looked at me and said, "What I meant, Jessica, was . . . um . . . I was wondering whether you'd mind a traveling companion."

"A traveling companion?"

She nodded. "I don't mean to impose myself on you and your trip. Believe me, I know how much this trip means to you, and I wouldn't for a second intrude. But considering what's happened to Wilimena—and that you're taking the same cruise as she did—on the same ship—it just seemed to me that—well, that maybe retracing her steps would help me come to grips with her disappearance."

"I, ah—"

Truth was, I was looking forward to the Alaska cruise as a means of getting away from everything and anything and basking in a week of solitude, with only whales, sea lions, otters, and eagles as traveling companions.

I looked to Seth, who knew exactly what I was thinking, not only because he knows me so well, but also because I'd spoken to him about my need to escape on a solo jaunt.

"Sounds like a good idea to me," Mike Cunniff said, running his hands through his hair. "Besides, Jessica, you seem to have a penchant for getting to the bottom of things rather quickly, especially when it involves—"

He'd almost said "murder," and I was glad he hadn't.

"What a great idea," Maureen said to me. "You'd have company and—"

"Mo and I talked about taking that cruise with you, Mrs. F.," Mort said, "but it's a bad time of the year for me."

Startled, I turned to him. "I didn't know you'd been considering coming," I said.

"It's probably not a good idea, me joining you," Kathy said.

"Oh, no, it's a—it's a good idea, Kathy. I just wasn't planning on traveling with anyone."

"I'd stay out of your hair, Jess," she said, "go my own way and try to find out what's happened to Willie." She laughed. "Chances are she met up with some handsome Mountie and decided to spend some time with him in Alaska."

"Or marry him?" Seth said.

Kathy sighed deeply.

"How many times has your sister been married?" Charlene asked.

"Let me see," Kathy said, counting on her fingers. "Four—I think! No, five."

Everyone had an opinion and a comment to make about Wilimena's penchant for tying the knot, but we stifled the temptation to express them. Wilimena's multiple marriages obviously satisfied a need of hers, and who were we to judge?

"Lovely dinner, as usual, Jessica," Seth said as they prepared to leave.

"Simple," I said.

"Always the best kind," Seth opined.

I saw them to the door and waved goodbye as they navigated a narrow path I'd shoveled through the snow dumped by the latest storm, and got into their vehicles. I locked up behind them, went to the kitchen and tidied up before undressing for bed and slipping into a fresh pair of pajamas, a robe, and slippers. I'd become sleepy during the latter part of the evening, but now found myself wide-awake. I added a log to the fireplace and sat in front of the yellow-orange flames casting pleasant shafts of light and shadow over the room. What consumed my thinking was, of course, Kathy Copeland's story about her sister's disappearance in Alaska. Had I been rude in not responding with enthusiasm to her suggestion that she accompany me on my Alaskan trip? I was certainly sympathetic to her worries, and her determination to do what she could to find Wilimena.

I suppose a sense of urgency was lacking in my mind because of Wilimena's history. I'd met her on a number of occasions when she'd come to Cabot Cove to visit her sister. Wilimena was a larger-than-life character, flamboyant and glamorous, so unlike Kathy, who was the salt of the earth, and dressed and acted like it. My friend wore flannel shirts, jeans, and workman's boots most of the time. She was a master gardener and excellent cook, and enjoyed the simple pleasures of a good book, a hike in the woods, or a fish fry down on the beach. She'd never married, which surprised me. Somewhere out there was a man who was missing out on a first-rate wife.

Wilimena, on the other hand, was flashy in a big-city sort of way, fond of glittery dresses that showed off her splendid figure, lots of jewelry, elaborate hairdos of varying hues, and a heavy, albeit effective use of makeup. Wilimena was, Kathy once told me, the younger of the sisters but only by a few years. Despite Wilimena's over-the-top personality, which could quickly wear you down, she was personable and likable, which her numerous husbands had obviously recognized, too.

I was pondering the events of the evening when the phone rang.

"Hello?"

"Jessica? It's Kathy."

"Oh, I'm glad you're home safe. How were the roads?"

"Not bad. Seth's a careful driver. He was a dear to offer to bring me."

"He's a dear about so many things."

"That he is. Jessica. Listen, I'm calling because I feel terrible about having suggested I go with you to Alaska."

"Why would you feel terrible?" I asked. "It was a sound suggestion. It's just that—"

"It was pushy of me, Jessica, and I apologize."

"No apologies needed, Kathy. As a matter of fact—"

"Yes?"

"I was just sitting here thinking about that very thing."

"You were?"

"Yes, and I think an apology is due from my end, too."

"For heaven's sake, why, Jessica?"

Excerpt from *PANNING FOR MURDER*

"Because you're obviously in need of some answers to Wilimena's disappearance, and taking the same cruise that she took might provide them. And, as Mike Cunniff said, I do seem to have a penchant for getting to the bottom of things. Besides, having company would be good for me. So, Kathy, I would be pleased to have you join me on the cruise."

"You would?"

"Yes, I would. I think you'd better call Susan Shevlin and see if she can get you space on the ship. It is, after all, very last minute."

"I'll do it first thing in the morning. You're sure, Jessica?"

I laughed. "Yes, I'm sure, Kathy. Get a booking in the morning, and let's meet for lunch to discuss the trip."

"Wonderful! Thanks so much, Jessica."

"My pleasure, Kathy. Now it's time for this lady to get to bed. See you tomorrow at Mara's. Twelve-thirty okay?"

"I'll be there."

The conversation with Kathy, and the decision I'd made, lifted the veil of ambivalence I'd been feeling, allowing fatigue once again to settle in. There's nothing like taking action when something unresolved is hanging over your head. I fell asleep quickly, with a smile on my face.